MELTDOWN

Andy McNab and Robert Rigby

First published in Great Britain by
Doubleday, an imprint of
Random House Children's Books 2007
This Large Print edition published by
BBC Audiobooks by arrangement with
Random House Children's Books 2009

ISBN: 978 1405 663236

British Library Cataloguing in Publication Data available

Printed and bound in Great Britain by
Antony Rowe Ltd., Chippenham, Wiltshire

GLOSSARY

ACA	*Alias cover address*
Build-up	*Training for an operation*
Contact	*In a fire fight with the enemy*
CQB	*Close quarter battle*
CT team	*Counter-terrorist team*
CTR	*Close target recce*
DMP	*Drug manufacturing plant*
End ex	*End exercise, but also used to end a mission or operation*
ERV	*Emergency rendezvous*
FAP	*Final assault position*
FARC	*Columbian drug traffickers*
FLIR	*Forward looking infra-red*
FOB	*Forward operating base*
GCHQ	*Government Communications Headquarters*
Int	*Intelligence*
IR	*Infra-red*
K	*Deniable operator*
Loadie	*Loadmaster*
A long	*Any rifle*
Mag	*A weapons magazine that holds the rounds*
Make ready a weapon	*To put a round (bullet) in the chamber, ready to be fired*
MOE	*Method of entry*
NVGs	*Night viewing goggles*
On stag	*On guard*

OP	*Observation post*
Op sec	*Operational security*
Pinged	*When someone is first seen*
Recce	*Reconnaissance*
The Regiment	*What SAS soldiers call the SAS*
RV	*Rendezvous (meeting place)*
A short	*Any pistol*
Sit rep	*Situation report*
SOP	*Standard operating procedure*
Stand to	*Get ready to be attacked*
UAV	*Unmanned aerial vehicle*
Yankees	*The team; the good guys*
X-rays	*Bad guys*

SURVEILLANCE TALK

Complete	*Inside any location—a car, building, etc.*
Foxtrot	*Walking*
Held	*Stopped but intending to move on—i.e. at traffic lights*
Mobile	*Driving*
Net	*The radio frequency the team talk on*
Roger	*OK or understood*
Stand by! Stand by!	*Informs the team something is happening*
Static	*Stopped*
The trigger	*Informs the team that the target is on the move*

Prologue

Glasgow

The thirty-minute team made the best use of the shadows as they approached their entry points and prepared for the attack. Close by, on the river Clyde, two tugs passed in opposite directions, their stubby bows pushing through the inky-black water.

The four snipers were giving cover with their 7.62mm suppressed longs from fire positions 200 metres from the target building, a single-storey warehouse. They watched all sides and the roof, ready to give warning instantly if they saw movement from within the target that would compromise the assault team as they made their entry.

Sniper one could see all four entry points and the assault groups moving in on them. He was giving constant updates to the entire team and the team commander, who was at the rear of the target with his signaller. He was the link between the team, the heli and London.

'Sierra One has no change. No light, no movement.'

Three of the four assault groups reached their entry points, and each MOE man carefully began attaching two 10x15cm pads of explosive to the doors by their adhesive undersides. The brick-sized rubber door-entry charges were stuck close to the door hinges inside the frame.

'Sierra One. No change.'

The calm, reassuring words gave the team confidence: everything was OK and someone had

1

eyes on them as they continued with their work.

They couldn't afford to cock up. Bringing in special forces to take action against non-terrorist targets on UK soil is a big deal, and permission for such action can only come from the very highest level.

The terrifying extent of the Meltdown crisis, with its threat to national and international security, had been kept from all but a very few. The mission to seek out and destroy the drug factory was urgent but it had to remain totally secret.

So when intelligence came in giving the location of a suspected DMP, immediate action had to be taken. The PM was consulted and asked for permission to 'stand to' the SAS counter-terrorist team from their base in Hereford. He gave the go-ahead.

The members of a thirty-minute team have to be able to reach camp within half an hour of being paged. As soon as the messages came through, just like volunteer firemen, they stopped whatever they were doing and got on the road.

At the same time a Chinook helicopter took off from its RAF base to pick up the team. By the time the guys had arrived at the camp and come into the crew room, where their gear was packed and waiting, the commanders were already writing down instructions on white marker boards.

The most important piece of information about the job appeared in big red capital letters:

HELI PICK-UP
COVERT OP UK

The team knew instantly that it was a civvies

2

clothes job, in boots and jeans, and that once the job was done, it would never exist on any database; they would act as if it had never happened.

Within thirty minutes the team, along with two Range Rovers, was airborne in the Chinook. Each member was armed with an MP5-SD, the suppressed version of the machine gun, and wore earphones and a mic so that their commander could relay orders for the attack as they flew north.

The Chinook landed three miles from the target area, on a desolate stretch of mudflats downstream. The wagons were swiftly unloaded, and within minutes the team was on its way to an area of abandoned warehouses and dockyards.

The whole operation to get the team to the target had taken less than four hours, and now three of the four groups were ready to attack, with sniper one keeping the commentary going.

'Sierra One has Red One, Two and Three ready.'

Red Four was taking the entry point furthest from their start position; slowly they crawled under the final window to reach the fire-escape door where they were going to make entry.

The MOE man moved to the right-hand side of the door and started to place the charges as the other three got into the assault position. Number one was just thirty centimetres away from the charges, with numbers two and three pressing up behind him. They had to be packed close together so that everyone was through the door as soon as possible to take on the x-rays inside.

The MOE man started to unroll the firing cable from the charges so that he could stand on the left-hand side of the door. He attached the electrical firing device to the cable and nodded to number one.

Only one thing remained to be done before the attack could begin. The final group's number two pulled the pin on an aerosol-can-sized 'flash-bang'. It was a grenade that exploded with blinding flashes and bangs, designed to attack the human eardrum and eyes so that its victims collapsed on the ground in agonizing pain. The assault groups had to go in at the same time as the flash-bang kicked off or they would lose the initiative. They had trained with the grenades over a long period of time and were now almost unaffected by flash-bangs.

The number two pushed his arm forward so that the flash-bang was in front of his number one's face; he knew everyone behind him was ready to go.

Sniper one could see that the final group was in position.

'Sierra One has Red Four ready. All groups ready.'

The team commander wasn't about to waste any more time or risk compromise by the third party or however many x-rays were inside the target.

'Hello all stations, I have control. Stand by! Stand by! Go!'

The four MOE guys pushed their buttons: ear-shattering explosions instantly blew away the doors. The teams stood their ground as wooden splinters were thrown into the air by the force of the charge, and the number twos threw in their flash-bangs as the number ones barged their way into the target.

The torches on the extra-thick suppressed

barrels of their MP5s penetrated the smoke and brick dust as flashes and bangs sent shock waves through their bodies, and the rest of the team followed them in. They kept their mouths open to stop their eardrums from bursting as the pressure waves from the flash-bangs filled the building; meanwhile their eyes hunted out targets.

There were none. Not a single x-ray.

And there was no sign of any manufacturing plant—the building looked completely empty.

Then, as Red Four moved further into the haze and the flash-bangs stopped, their number one came across a dead body. Well dead.

The guy looked as though he was in his early twenties. He lay flat on his back in a pool of blood which had burst from his mouth, eyes and ears. His face was bloated and contorted into a twisted mask of agony and fear.

Number one reached into his pocket and pulled out a camera. He took some photos of the blood-soaked body, then grabbed it and began to drag it from the building.

Within seconds, news of the failed attack had been relayed to London and a decision was taken.

It was time for a complete change of tactics.

OPERATION MELTDOWN—FORMATION OF MELTDOWN 'TASK FORCE'

Background and current situation
Meltdown (also known as an 'M' or a 'Melt'): chemical/designer drug first appeared in UK and Europe spring 2006. *Known to have been created and manufactured in UK.* The tablets (marked with a distinctive 'M') are being manufactured and distributed at an alarmingly quick rate: manufacturing site(s) and distribution method(s) unknown.

Effects
Without doubt, and for numerous reasons, this is potentially the *most dangerous chemical drug ever created*. Apparently called Meltdown because slowing of the heartbeat leads to a gradual feeling of relaxation, tranquillity and complete well-being. However, prolonged use appears to cause completely opposite effect: *uncontrollable rage and extreme violent behaviour*. The drug is highly addictive. Laboratory tests indicate that Meltdown causes breakdown of brain tissue and 'meltdown' of internal organs. Autopsy on the only known death (male, aged 23 years) directly attributed to continued

use of Meltdown appears to confirm all indications. The victim, an army dropout of known previous A1 health, suffered brain tissue destruction, extensive damage to liver and kidneys, and abnormal enlargement of heart muscle. Autopsy report concludes that at the moment of death the victim's heart literally 'burst'. Full autopsy report attached (Doc: MDO/574688C).

Chemical make-up, formula and manufacture
While our scientists have identified the chemical 'ingredients', to date the specific formula and manufacturing method remain completely elusive. In layman's terms, the simplest analogy is with Coca-Cola, in that we know what is in Meltdown but we do not know how, or by what process it is constructed.

National and international implications
Specially convened government think-tank, in conjunction with our European partners, predicts that if Meltdown is permitted to spread at current rate, health services throughout Europe could go into overload within two years, and violence on the streets will reach uncontrollable levels, leading to the implementation of martial law. *The think-tank also stresses the danger of the Meltdown formula falling into the hands of a terrorist organization. Worst-case scenarios include the possibility of*

8

Meltdown being converted into liquid form to contaminate public water supply or into a highly concentrated aerosol form for use in confined spaces, e.g. public transport. Full think-tank report attached (Doc: GTT/829745a).

National and international security situation
The added threat of potential terrorist interest/involvement in this drug dictates that we continue to keep the full effects of Meltdown unknown to the general public for as long as possible. *Note: This instruction comes from the highest possible level, with unanimous agreement from European partners.* Public, press, media, police and other arms of the security services *must* remain ignorant of the operation.

Current operational situation (UK)
Total failure of previous raid on suspected DMP and lack of further strong intelligence has led to a rethink on tactics and strategy and the planned formation of a *Meltdown Task Force*. Surveillance operations continue, targeting Meltdown users and dealers. These have resulted in some new leads, but a highest-level decision has been made to take no further direct action until the Meltdown Task Force is operational. Vitally important that task force becomes operational immediately.

Operational aims

To infiltrate organization producing drug, destroy manufacturing plants, identify and eliminate European distribution network and contacts. *To eliminate all those knowing the Meltdown formula and to destroy formula itself.*

CLASSIFIED—CLASSIFIED—CLASSIFIED

1

Canada

'Get to the ERV!'

Danny knew enough about SOPs by now to follow his grandfather's order without argument.

He didn't wait to collect anything; everything he would need for the next few hours and, if necessary, the next few days was hidden at the ERV.

He slipped noiselessly away from the wooden cabin by the edge of the vast dark lake and disappeared into the towering trees. The ERV was a kilometre into the forest and Danny's first objective was to get there and wait. For six hours. After that, if his grandfather, Fergus, didn't turn up, there were other plans to put into action. But that was for later.

*   *   *

Inside the cabin, Fergus peered through an open but shuttered window at the mud track, which rose gradually for 150 metres. At the top of the incline sat a stationary black 4x4.

Fergus had already taken the hunting rifle with a telescopic sight off the wall bracket above the fireplace and then lifted the bolt before gently pulling it back to reveal the shiny brass of a round already in the chamber. He pushed the bolt home and didn't bother to apply the safety catch.

He took aim through the shutters and focused on

11

the 4x4. The powerful sight easily picked out the features of the person behind the wheel, a face that Fergus instantly recognized.

He was surprised; he hadn't expected them to come like this. He had anticipated a sudden hit by a full team. But he was calm as he calculated all the possibilities: his years in the Regiment and his later work as a 'K' meant he was always ready for any eventuality.

He placed the cross-hairs dead centre on the face. It would be a simple shot, as easy as a fairground shooting gallery.

* * *

Danny reached the ERV and got straight to work without even pausing for breath.

He had no official military or intelligence service training, yet he operated like a professional—but then he'd had a good teacher, the best. And Danny had learned quickly. He'd had to in order to stay alive.

Now it seemed as if their lives were in danger again, but like his grandfather, Danny had learned not to panic in a crisis.

They'd chosen the spot for the ERV because of the good line of sight in every direction and because the huge fallen tree made a perfect marker. Close to the massive trunk lay a chunk of flat grey stone. Rocks like this dotted the landscape so it looked perfectly natural.

Danny shifted the stone to one side and cleared away the leaf litter. He used his hands to dig into the soil beneath and soon unearthed two black plastic bags just below the surface. Inside each bag was a day sack packed with tinned food, bottled water, fresh clothes and a wad of cash.

Quickly and methodically, Danny removed the day sacks from the protective bags and checked the contents, keeping a watch all the time for anyone who might be approaching through the forest.

But no one came near. The only sounds were birdsong and the light breeze that shivered through the treetops. Danny refilled the hole he had dug and replaced the leaf litter and the flat stone. When he and Fergus left, there would be no sign of them ever having been there.

Danny stood up and checked the area where he had worked. It was just as it had been when he'd arrived. His grandfather would be pleased, *if* he ever reached the ERV. They had often discussed their contingency escape plans, and even though Danny wasn't panicking, he was worried.

All he could do now was wait. If his grandfather hadn't shown up when the six hours were up, he was on his own. But he wasn't thinking about that, not yet.

He sat down with his back to the tree trunk and peered out through the trees in the direction he had come from. Nothing. No one. He glanced upwards: the sky was as grey and cold as the rocks that lay all around.

For all he knew he might never see his grandfather again. He might already be dead. They had known each other for little more than a year, but in that year so much had happened. They'd spent much of it on the run, battling to clear Fergus of the false accusations levelled against him.

Now they were on the run again. Things hadn't gone well between Danny and Fergus in the four months since their escape from New York. They'd become almost like strangers again.

Danny sighed. 'He's always making me run away. Like I'm still a kid, like he still doesn't trust me. I could have stayed and helped him.'

He stared through the trees again, knowing in his heart that his grandfather had been protecting him. Fergus couldn't run any more; two gunshot wounds in the same leg meant that swift movement was impossible, whereas Danny was an experienced cross-country runner. Fergus had stood his ground to fight so that his grandson could escape.

Danny sighed again. 'He's probably gone and got himself killed.'

2

Fergus had almost smiled as he watched the small, elderly man step from the 4x4 and begin buttoning up his overcoat.

He knew the procedure. Through the rifle's telescopic sight, Fergus watched him raise both arms on either side of his body to signal that he was about to approach. And as he started walking down the long track, Fergus covered every step.

Although the little man appeared harmless and seemed to be alone, Fergus was too seasoned a campaigner to take anything for granted. He watched and waited, his finger resting on the trigger of the hunting rifle.

Far down the track, the man's first few steps were hesitant, but as he got closer he seemed to grow in confidence. He couldn't see Fergus or Danny, but he knew perfectly well that, somewhere, a weapon was being aimed at his head. And as he neared the cabin, he became increasingly certain that Fergus was going to let him speak, rather than dropping him before he got the chance to open his mouth.

Fifteen metres from the cabin he stopped. He spoke loudly and clearly, still with both arms outstretched.

'Good morning, Mr Watts. You have my word that I'm completely alone, and unarmed. I'd be most grateful if you would permit me to lower my arms and join you in the, er . . . cabin.'

There was no reply.

He sighed. 'I'm too old for all this, Mr Watts. I just want to talk. That's all.'

*   *   *

Danny checked his watch. He'd been at the ERV for nearly two hours and there was still no sign of his grandfather.

As the minutes passed, he grew more and more worried and started thinking about going off his grandfather's precious SOPs by carefully working his way back towards the cabin to see for himself what was going on.

Fergus would be furious, but Danny was used to that. Since they'd made it to Canada there had been moments of anger and long silences, with neither of them capable of putting right what had gone wrong.

Danny's thoughts turned to Elena. She'd been

15

his best friend, his closest confidante, and much more than that: he'd loved her. He still did. He knew it more every day. And he missed her.

He was thinking about the way they had talked and laughed and planned their futures when he suddenly heard the slight crack of a twig breaking.

He looked up. It was his grandfather.

Fergus saw the look of relief on his grandson's face. He smiled. 'What have I told you about staying alert at all times? You should have pinged me several minutes ago.'

Danny managed a slight smile of his own. 'I was . . . thinking.'

'Yeah,' said Fergus, nodding. 'It seems we've got a bit more thinking to do.'

Danny stood up. 'Who was it—in the four by four?'

'Dudley.' He saw his grandson's surprised stare. 'You'd better come and hear what he's got to say.'

*   *   *

Dudley was one of the top men in MI5. He had been behind Operation Black Star, which had ended so calamitously in New York with the death of Elena. And he had been in ultimate charge of the earlier plan to eliminate both Fergus and Danny. It was not surprising that they were wary of him.

He had come up with the new plan for Operation Meltdown. It was daring and risky, but Dudley didn't care about that. Not any more. *They* had talked him into delaying his retirement; *they* would have to go along with his unorthodox methods. He had been looking forward to retirement, but the

16

sense of being needed and the heavy hint at a possible knighthood if the vital operation was successful were ample compensation for the delay.

Dudley knew little about designer drugs, but when the think-tank report labelled Meltdown the most dangerous concoction ever to have come out of an illegal laboratory, he reasoned that drastic measures were required. Thousands, possibly hundreds of thousands, of lives were at risk, and there was the added dire warning of the Meltdown formula falling into the hands of terrorist organizations.

Operation Meltdown would be a complex, dangerous and dirty operation, and Dudley had decided that the person he wanted to lead his task force was Fergus Watts.

3

Dudley slowly stirred a steaming mug of thick black coffee. He looked tired; the flight from the UK and the long drive had taken their toll. He sipped at the coffee and felt the surge of caffeine.

Having given Danny the broad details of the growing Meltdown crisis and told him about his proposed special task force, Dudley had suddenly seemed very tired. He'd unbuttoned the overcoat he always wore and asked for a coffee.

While Fergus made the brew, Dudley glanced at Danny, who was turning over in his mind everything that had been said. Whatever decisions were made, Fergus wouldn't make them alone.

'Why us?' said Danny.

17

'Firstly, because of your grandfather's vast experience in combating drugs traffickers. FARC in Colombia, the IRA drug runners in Northern Ireland. He's been inside those organizations; he knows how they operate. That knowledge will be invaluable.'

Danny shrugged; it wasn't enough to have brought Dudley all the way from his comfortable office in London.

'And then there are the people we're targeting,' Dudley added quickly. 'They're vain and arrogant. They enjoy the champagne lifestyle and they like to mix with the famous or even the infamous. They will undoubtedly be drawn to high-profile characters like yourselves once their own problems begin.'

'High profile?' asked Danny. 'Us?'

'Oh, you will be,' said Dudley, reaching into an inside pocket of his overcoat. He pulled out a folded sheet of paper, opened it and placed it on the table for Danny to read. It was a mock-up of a newspaper headline.

TRAITOR REVEALED
AS SECRET HERO

'That's one of my own,' said Dudley, shrugging modestly. The hot coffee had had a reviving effect. 'But I'm sure my experts will come up with even more tantalizing headlines, as well as the stories to go with them.'

Danny looked over at his grandfather. 'I don't get it.'

'Let him explain,' answered Fergus quietly.

Dudley swiftly outlined his plan. 'Your

grandfather has a history. I want to use that history to draw in our targets.'

'But why? Why not use one of your own men?'

'Because there isn't time, Danny. The Meltdown crisis is spiralling out of control. There's no time to create a believable legend for some non-existent hero. Your grandfather's story is all there on the record, in black and white.'

Danny listened as Dudley explained that he was already preparing a carefully orchestrated press campaign. A deliberately leaked MI5 report would reveal that Fergus had played a massive part in halting a worldwide teenage suicide bombing campaign, after being secretly recruited for Operation Black Star.

He would be acclaimed as a national hero and, as a result, the government would have no option but to publicly 'pardon' him for his previous crimes against the country. Fergus had long been accused of being a traitor, of selling out to the FARC drug barons in Colombia when he was meant to be working towards their destruction. They all knew it was a false accusation, but it would remain on the record.

'But he's innocent,' said Danny quickly. 'You know that. We proved it before the Black Star operation.'

Dudley nodded indulgently. 'Of course I know it. But we want our targets to think exactly the opposite. We want them to think that he's guilty; that he's corrupt, perfectly willing to enter into a shady deal if the money is right. That's what will make him attractive to them.'

'But why should—?'

'Let me finish, please?' said Dudley, holding up

19

his hands. 'We'll make it absolutely clear that while we're grateful for everything your grandfather has done, he can never again be employed by any government organization. That's important.'

He sat back, looking pleased with his plan. He raised his eyebrows, inviting Danny's questions.

'These targets you keep talking about, who are they?'

The elderly man shook his head. 'I'm afraid that information must remain classified until I know that you're in.'

Danny pushed away his chair and stood up. 'I've had enough of all this classified shit.' He glared at his grandfather. 'And operational secrets.' He started to walk towards the door.

'Wait, Danny!' said Fergus. As Danny stopped by the door, Fergus fixed his eyes on Dudley. 'The targets? Who are they?'

Dudley sighed. 'They're young brothers—twins by the name of Headingham.'

'So, if you've got a name, why don't you just go in and bust them?'

'Because it's not the right way, I'm certain of that now. There are no new clues to the location of the DMP—we had a task force go into a warehouse we suspected was manufacturing drugs, but it was absolutely empty; we don't understand where and how they're making Meltdown. And the distribution network is also a complete mystery. I'm absolutely sure there's at least one much bigger fish somewhere in Europe who we need to identify and net. I'm convinced that the only way to get everything we want is by infiltrating the twins' set-up. But it must be done quickly.'

Danny was still by the door. He leaned back

against the wall. *'We?'* He nodded towards his grandfather but continued speaking to Dudley. 'I can see why you want him, but where do I fit in?'

Fergus answered the question before Dudley could reply. 'We're a team, Danny. I'm not going anywhere without you.'

'We'll mention in the newspaper reports that you also played an important part in Operation Black Star,' said Dudley quickly. 'You could be very useful.'

Danny laughed cynically. 'Useful? What you really mean is, if you want my granddad, you have to take me too. Yeah, that's really useful. And there's something else you haven't mentioned, isn't there?'

Dudley knew what was coming but he waited for Danny to continue.

'What about Deveraux? Is she part of this?'

Dudley sighed. 'You know, I really am truly sorry about your friend, Miss—'

'Yeah, right,' snapped Danny. He didn't want to discuss Elena with Dudley. After all, *he* had played his part in her death, even if he hadn't pulled the trigger. 'Deveraux . . . is she part of it?'

'Not at all. Miss Deveraux is no longer with the Security Service.'

'So where is she?'

'I think she was expecting to take over my job. When that didn't happen, she returned to the Secret Intelligence Service, concentrating on overseas operations rather than our problems at home. I'm told she's doing extremely well. This is *my* initiative, and if you take the job, you'll be working directly under my control. When it's over, if you want to, you can walk away, your names

21

finally and completely cleared. You'll be free to do whatever you want and go wherever you want to go. No more looking over your shoulder to see who might be following.'

Fergus put down the coffee mug he had been nursing and looked at Dudley. 'Danny and me need to have a few words alone.' He nodded towards the coffee pot that was still bubbling on the stove. 'Help yourself.'

*   *   *

It was cold outside the cabin and the shadows were already beginning to lengthen. They walked towards the lake and Fergus said nothing until they were well out of earshot of the cabin.

'It gives us a chance, Danny. To get this done and then make a new start.'

'Because we're a *team*?' said Danny sarcastically, echoing the words his grandfather had used in the cabin. 'Well, that's what I thought until you let me and Elena down in New York. If you'd told us you knew that Deveraux had killed Elena's dad, then Elena would never have been there. We'd have got out, and Elena would still be alive.'

'*All right!*' said Fergus angrily. 'I did what I thought was right at the time! Op sec! That's the way it works. And if you can't get that into your head, then you might as well get a job stacking shelves in a supermarket.'

Danny was ready to fight back as his own anger boiled over. 'Yeah, well maybe that'd be better than being stuck here with you! I'm only here because of you! Doing nothing. Walking up and down this poxy lake until I know every rock and every tree!'

He picked up a stone and hurled it as hard as he could, far out into the lake. They saw the splash as it landed and the ripples that went spilling out in every direction.

'So this is a way out of here,' Fergus suggested mildly. 'Let's do it.'

Danny kept his eyes on the water as he spoke again, more quietly now. 'Why should we trust Dudley, after everything that's happened before?'

'Because he's here. Once they found out where we were, they could have taken us, Danny; sent a full team to eliminate us. Dudley's here because he needs us.'

'He needs *you*,' said Danny, turning to look at his grandfather. 'I'm not important.'

'You are to me.' Fergus looked closely at his grandson. 'We have to move on, Danny. It's no good living in the past. Like Dudley said, we do this job and then get out.'

'And what about Deveraux? Do you really believe she's out of the picture?'

Fergus nodded. 'I don't think even Dudley would ever consider putting us back together with Deveraux.'

When they went back into the cabin, Dudley was still sitting exactly where they'd left him, staring morosely into an empty coffee mug.

They sat at the table and Fergus got straight down to business. 'So after all this "hero" stuff in the newspapers, what then?'

Dudley nodded and then smiled. 'We reveal, in a follow-up story, that you are setting up your own independent security consultancy. That will most certainly attract the twins' interest when phase two of the operation begins.'

Before they went into the details of the operation, Fergus wanted to get a couple more things straight. 'I choose the rest of the team.'

It was nothing less than Dudley had expected. 'Agreed.'

'And Danny's not ready. He's never worked in a team. He needs a build-up.'

Dudley stood up and brushed down his overcoat. 'We have little time; the Meltdown crisis is like a ticking time bomb. Ten days maximum, but I need *you* on the ground as soon as possible.'

Fergus looked at his grandson, and when he spoke, there was a hint of pride in his voice. 'Danny's a quick learner.'

4

SAS training area near Hereford, England

They used to call them the 'killing houses', but back in the 1990s, when the press picked up on the term, the Regiment had decided to become politically correct. Now they were known simply by the official name, CQB houses.

At first sight the training area looked like a bizarre cross between a small but deserted town and a war zone. There were houses and blocks of red-brick flats alongside parked aircraft and a variety of vehicles. It all appeared bleak, abandoned and haphazard, but everything had a very specific purpose.

Fergus had wanted Danny to get specialist

training and he was getting it. Like a non-swimmer thrown in at the deep end, Danny's only options were to sink or swim, and he was swimming—or at least keeping his head above water. It was tough, but it was meant to be. The Regiment had a saying: *Train hard; fight easy. Train easy; fight hard—and die.*

Danny's eighteenth birthday had come and gone while they were in Canada, and as far as Fergus was concerned, as his grandson was now part of a professional team, his build-up had to be as hard and tough as any SAS trooper's.

So the instructors were taking little heed of Danny's age and inexperience. They had a job to do and they were doing it. If Danny didn't come up to the mark, it wouldn't be down to them.

Fergus wasn't even around to oversee Danny's progress. He was up in Manchester working on phase two of Operation Meltdown; the phase one newspaper campaign had already taken place, with the predicted mass-media interest.

Meanwhile, Danny was at Hereford with the two other members of the task force. Their cover story was that they were working for Fergus's security consultancy company, and Fergus had insisted that at least one member of the team must have genuine experience of working for such a set-up.

Phil Reddington was ex-Regiment. He was ten years younger than Fergus but their paths had crossed many times. Fergus rated him, and that was a good enough reference for Dudley. He had not been difficult to poach from his employers, a private military company, once Fergus had mentioned the fee for the one-off job. He could always go back when it was over; the best guys were always in demand.

He had been working in Baghdad, guarding VIPs, for the best part of two years, watching the locals rip themselves apart as most of the country continued its downward spiral towards total anarchy, with the coalition forces helpless to do anything but dodge the bullets and pick up the pieces. Sometimes it was innocent bystanders, sometimes insurgents, and sometimes—the worst times for guys like Phil—it was friends. Guys like him.

But Phil didn't trouble himself too much with politics, or deciding on the rights and wrongs of situations; usually he was too busy making sure he stayed alive. And getting on with his job. His attitude to life was 'never explain and never complain'. He kept himself to himself, but Fergus liked that.

Dudley had recommended the fourth member of the team, even though Fergus had the final word on selection. His name was Leroy Simmons, and at just twenty-five he was already highly regarded in the Security Service. Fergus had met him, grilled him and recognized quickly that Dudley's assessment was correct. He was in; the team was complete.

Now Phil, Leroy and Danny were being put through their paces in Hereford.

Phil had little to learn—he could probably have taught most of the instructors a thing or two—but it was important that the three got to know and trust each other, and the best way to achieve this was to train together, working as a team. Fergus also wanted Phil there to keep a watchful eye on Danny and, to a lesser extent, on Leroy, who was being taught weapon-handling drills he'd never learned with MI5.

The ten-day build-up was now virtually over, and Danny was knackered, physically, mentally and even emotionally. There was so much to take in. But he'd not only hugely increased his personal fitness levels; he'd also been fast-tracked through both standard and advanced driving courses, and improved his street craft and trade craft, which Fergus had spent more than a year trying to drum into him.

There had been MOE work, where Danny had learned how to covertly break into locations so that he could carry out close target recces.

And there had been extensive weapons training: if Danny was old enough to carry a weapon, he was old enough to use it. And there was no point in him learning how to handle a weapon unless he was willing and able to pull the trigger—to save his own life, or someone else's. He had to accept that if ever he pointed a weapon at someone, he had to shoot to kill. So 'Show your hands or I will shoot' could never be merely a threat. If he said it, he had to mean it.

He'd become familiar with a comprehensive range of weaponry, ranging from the latest 9mm pistols and 5.56mm assault rifles to the sort of stuff used by street gangs—revolvers and shotguns.

Now Danny was embarking on a final day of tests. He was holding a 9mm Sig semi-automatic pistol. The weapon already had a familiar feel in his hands, and so far he had acquitted himself well on the ranges and in various exercises.

But this task was going to be very different from anything he'd done before. He was about to burst into a room and take on a number of life-size cut-out x-rays with rapid double taps to the head.

Danny had learned new words as well as the skills that went with them. *X-rays* were the enemy, while *yankees* were those on his own side. He was already familiar with the term 'the third party' from his time with Fergus. The third party was Joe or Josephine Public—anyone who was unaware of what was going on around them on the streets. These code words were used by the SAS to make information sent over the radio net easier to understand.

As far as this exercise was concerned, Danny would know if the rounds had hit the x-rays because each one had a red inflated balloon filled with red chalk dust pinned to the head.

It sounded simple enough, but there was an added complication. Amongst the targets was a real person: Phil Reddington was sitting on a chair somewhere in the room. And on top of that, Danny had no advance knowledge of where the x-rays would be sited. They might be directly in front of Phil or just inches to the side.

Phil's life was literally in Danny's hands.

The Regiment uses such exercises to build confidence and trust, and as Danny waited for the order from his instructor to go, he was desperately hoping that Phil's apparent confidence in him would not be misplaced.

The burly SAS instructor looked at Danny closely. 'Remember, always head shots.'

Danny nodded.

'No good nodding, son. I want to know why.'

'Because the x-rays could be wearing body armour.'

28

'Correct. Anyone can get hold of it these days. And not only that: if you come up against someone high on drugs, it might take three or four double taps to the body before the stupid bastard realizes he's dead.'

Danny smiled thinly at the even thinner joke. He'd got used to the very particular brand of humour that ran through the place. The guys here were being trained in the art of killing, and the terrible jokes and camaraderie helped them all to keep a sense of sanity as they went about their deadly business.

'A double tap to the head will make sure they drop like liquid,' added the instructor as he poked Danny's head twice with an index finger. He nodded at the closed door. 'Your mate's in there. Make sure he's still your mate when it's all over.' He moved back a little, ready to give the order to begin. 'Stand by! Stand by!'

Danny braced himself and held the pistol in both hands.

'Go!'

Danny sucked in a breath, raised his right foot and kicked open the door; with his pistol in the aim and both eyes open wide so as to assimilate as much information as possible, he ran into the room, taking in the immediate threat as he entered.

There were two x-rays to the left, one two metres away, the other further. He double tapped the closest one, the main threat, and the weapon's report thudded in his ears as the walls bounced back the short, sharp, high-velocity sounds. The balloon exploded and sent red dust into the air as Danny kept moving forward, his eyes already fixed

29

on the head of the next x-ray.

Danny's mind went into slow motion, even though he knew he was operating quickly. The target became blurry: both his eyes were focusing on the pistol's foresight as it lined up on a female x-ray's head. With only the front pad of his finger on the trigger he squeezed off a double tap, short and sharp, and the balloon disintegrated in a cloud of red dust.

His head flicked right. A figure was sitting behind a table. Beyond that was another. He saw a flash of red on the first figure and kept focused on it, turning his body and weapon towards the target, bringing it in line with the head as he raised the weapon into the aim. The target went blurry as he focused once again on the foresight and tightened the pressure on the trigger.

But something was wrong. The red was on the target's chest, not the head. It had to be Phil!

Danny kept moving forward towards the target behind Phil.

'Get down! Down!'

He needed a clear shot. Phil dropped to the floor as commanded, and Danny double tapped the final x-ray, about seven metres away from him. His first shots missed, and he kept double tapping and moving towards the target until red dust exploded into the room.

The instructor stopped the exercise. 'Stop! Unload!'

It was over. It had taken no longer than ten seconds. Danny's heart was thumping as the adrenalin pumped through his body. He could feel his fingers trembling slightly on the trigger of the Sig as he squeezed off the action after unloading.

30

His ears were ringing as they struggled to cope with the high-velocity noise he had created.

Phil Reddington got up, looking completely untroubled apart from the red chalk-dust that covered his hair. It was as though he'd sat through nothing more threatening than a thunderstorm. But Phil was old school; he gave little away. His focus was on the next part of his job, which was to debrief Danny.

'Not bad,' he said with a shrug. 'But you took too many rounds to drop that fella behind me, didn't you?'

Danny nodded. 'Yeah. Yeah, sorry.'

Phil indicated the chair. 'Take a seat, son,' he said with a smile. 'It's your turn now.'

*   *   *

Danny and Lee, as Leroy preferred to be known, got on well from the outset, which was good news because they were going to be operating as partners for much of the time. And Danny was glad that one member of the team was a lot closer to his own age.

Now they were sitting together in a vehicle on a firing range. Their objective was to carry out an anti-ambush drill, with Danny at the wheel of the Audi A4 and Lee in the passenger seat.

Danny had proved to be an instinctive and fearless driver, without being reckless, which at the speeds he'd been travelling would soon have proved fatal. He'd advanced smoothly from the basics of cockpit drills and getting the most from the vehicle by the use of the gears, through to intensive high-speed work and then offensive and defensive driving, which was carried out on the firing ranges.

The high-speed work took place on the roads between Hereford and Bristol—everything from country lanes to forest tracks, dual carriageways, motorway, and the city of Bristol itself.

Now Danny was ready for his final test.

He was far from what anyone in the Regiment would describe as the finished article, but there was no more time. He'd had a couple of run-ins with Phil Reddington, who was almost as hard a taskmaster as his grandfather—maybe that was one of the reasons why Fergus had wanted him on the team.

Danny sat behind the wheel of the A4 as they prepared to go. Lee's MP5 was in the footwell, covered by a coat, just as it would have been if they were out on the street. The automatic machine gun was an excellent car weapon. Its collapsible butt made concealment easy, but the 9mm high-powered rounds could easily rip through a vehicle windscreen.

Lee looked at Danny. 'You ready then?'

Danny pulled his seat belt across his body, but he didn't click it home. On operations, they didn't wear seat belts because of the time it took to unbuckle them. Even SAS troops under fire have forgotten to unbuckle themselves, losing precious seconds in getting out of a vehicle to take on the enemy.

That was why Danny and Lee had Velcro glued to the buckle and holder. The seat belt had to look as if it were being worn correctly so that they blended in with the third party.

Danny secured the belt and nodded. 'Yep.'

He pressed the send button on the gear stick and spoke into the concealed microphone on the dashboard.

'That's Delta One mobile.'

Danny shoved the gear stick into first and got his foot down; soon he was doing seventy mph along the narrow track, cutting through the woods towards the range. The trees on either side became a green blur, and when Danny took it over a rise, the A4 flew into the air, the engine roaring. Lee pushed his feet into the footwell to support himself as they touched down again and the range came into view about half a mile away.

Danny hit the gear stick pressel, taking a sharp bend as the track cut across fields.

'That's Delta One approaching the range.'

Lee's MP5 was still in the footwell; he wouldn't draw down the weapon until it was needed. Everything was played as if it were for real.

The A4 was still doing seventy as it entered the range. Ahead, Danny saw a tall berm—a thick man-made earthworks, five metres high on three sides of the square, so that rounds could be fired to the sides as well as forward.

In front of the vehicle were six wooden targets— men and women in civvies, all of them holding weapons. An explosion directly in front of them lifted a fireball into the air and Danny hit the brake and pressed the send pressel.

'Contact! Contact! Wait out!'

Lee had already raised his MP5; he pulled out the butt before ramming it into his shoulder and pushing down the safety. The A4 skidded towards the enemy; Danny's feet were pushed hard down onto the brake and clutch and he fought to keep

33

the vehicle straight as Lee started firing.

The windscreen shattered and the automatic weapon's empty casings bounced off the roof and down onto Danny. As the A4 screeched to a standstill, Lee was still firing and giving Danny some cover.

'Go, Danny! Go!'

Danny didn't need telling twice. He pushed open the door and launched himself out of the vehicle, the Velcro ripping away and freeing the seat belt. Rolling onto the ground, he pulled out his pistol from the pancake holster on his right hip and began firing from beneath the door.

'Go! Go! Go!'

Instead of rolling out and taking cover, Lee dropped his MP5 and empty mag to the ground, drew down his own pistol and moved forward. He stopped in front of the vehicle, putting down rounds into the x-rays.

'Go!'

It was Danny's cue to move again. He stopped firing and leaped to his feet, running past the front of the A4 until he was a couple of metres ahead. He dropped down onto one knee and took on the x-rays.

'Go!'

Lee had started moving forward as soon as he heard Danny firing. They were taking the fight to the enemy; it was known as 'fire and manoeuvre', meaning that there was always someone firing while the other moved. They were working well together.

Danny reached his next position and pulled the trigger. Nothing happened. The top slide was held back because he was out of ammo.

'Stoppage!'

Lee stopped moving and put down fire; Danny pushed the mag-release catch with his thumb and the empty mag fell to the ground. He pulled a full one from his jacket pocket, reloaded and released the top slide catch with his thumb as he ran on. It rammed forward, picking up a round at the top of the mag and loading it.

Stopping just a metre short of the targets, Danny was close enough to put double taps into their heads as Lee ran up to join him; they continued firing until they ran out of ammo.

They unloaded their weapons and glanced at each other. They'd done well. All targets were punctured with their double taps and they had put down fire continuously as they moved forward.

Phil had watched the whole exercise, and for once there was a slight smile on his face.

That evening he called Fergus in Manchester. 'We're done. As ready as we'll ever be.'

'How did Danny get on?'

Fergus waited while Phil considered his reply, and when it came, it was almost exactly what he had expected.

'He can be cocky, and headstrong, and sometimes he thinks he knows it all without being told. But he's done good. And I've got to admit, he's a tough little bastard. How's phase two going?'

Fergus smiled into the telephone. 'Going to plan. See you in Manchester.'

5

Manchester, England

'We've checked you out, Mr Watts.'

'I would have been worried if you hadn't.'

'Ex-SAS. More medals than David Beckham. Quite a hero, before it all went wrong.'

'If you've done all your checks, you'll know that I've been officially pardoned.'

'Oh, we have. We know *everything* about you; we followed the stories with great interest. You're famous. We like that.'

Fergus and the Headingham twins were standing in a large yard enclosed by a high fence topped with barbed wire. The stench of petrol and charred rubber and leather hung in the air as they inspected the remains of four burned-out coaches. They were totally destroyed—nothing more than blackened skeletons.

Two pristine coaches with matching black gloss livery and darkened windows stood well away from the wrecked vehicles; across the yard a couple of young guys leaned against the wall of a huge workshop with open double doors. Inside, another coach was being steam-cleaned.

Fergus was meeting Teddy and Will Headingham for the first time. He'd seen the surveillance pics and read the int: identical twins, twenty-two, privileged background, same prep school, public school and university—Oxford, of course—same degree in chemistry, now partners in business together, running a fleet of luxury coaches to football matches on the continent—at least that was their legit business.

But Fergus was more interested in his own first impressions of the Headingham twins. Up close, it really was almost impossible to tell one from the other. From his manner and in the way he dominated the conversation, Teddy was obviously the senior partner. He was maybe a couple of centimetres taller than his brother, but they were both strikingly good-looking, tall and slim, with blond hair and piercing, cold blue eyes. And both were dressed in lightweight, stone-coloured Paul Smith suits.

They looked immaculate, completely out of place in the coach yard, unlike the two young guys leaning against the workshop wall, who were staring at Fergus as though they were just itching for the signal to do him some serious damage.

Fergus nodded towards them. 'That your own muscle? Bit young, aren't they?'

'One might say that perhaps you're a bit old, Mr Watts,' said Teddy. 'And hardly in prime physical condition. I couldn't help but notice the limp. They didn't mention that in the newspapers.'

'I get the job done.'

'Oh, indeed you do. You're an expert at what you do—that's why we contacted you. And as for our own security team, they may be young, but they too get the job done.'

Fergus looked back at the burned-out coaches. 'So I see.'

Teddy's pale face coloured a little. '*Touché*, Mr Watts.'

Fergus was still looking at the blackened remains. 'So, who did this?' he asked.

'We've no idea,' said Will quickly. 'Possibly business rivals.'

Fergus almost smiled. 'Bit drastic. And you say this is the third incident?'

'The first time, when my car was taken and burned out, we thought it was just joyriders,' Will explained. 'But then the upstairs office was trashed. And now this. And all in the last two weeks.'

Fergus turned and looked at him. 'I didn't know the ticket-sales business was so cut-throat.'

'We do a lot more than sell tickets,' said Will defensively. 'We provide exclusive luxury packages for sporting events. Travel, tickets and hotel accommodation.'

'Yeah, you can spare me the sales pitch.' Fergus turned to Teddy. 'All I need to know is if you want me to review your security. But like I told you, I don't come cheap.'

Teddy nodded. 'Let's go and talk.'

Fergus glanced over to where the two heavies were still attempting to look menacing. 'You think they'll let us in?'

'This place is for the workers,' said Teddy dismissively. 'We'll go to our apartment. It's more private, and somewhat more salubrious.' He took the keys of a BMW 7-series from his jacket pocket and nodded towards the vehicle, which was parked close to the main gates. 'I'll lead the way. And as we're still waiting for Will's replacement car, perhaps you won't mind if he travels with you.'

6

The listening device had been fitted into a back tooth, replacing an earlier filling in Fergus's mouth. It looked exactly like a normal filling but was actually a tiny microphone powered by the electricity in Fergus's body.

The device had originally been developed for use by the American Drug Enforcement Agency, whose undercover operatives needed to be able to record their encounters with drug dealers for evidence in court. A receiving station had to be positioned within a hundred metres, but the suitcase-sized piece of kit could easily be set up in a car or a nearby building.

Fergus was behind the wheel of a new Land Rover Discovery. It was the right sort of vehicle for the job, but then nothing had been left to chance; everything had to be right.

As soon as he pulled away from the yard, the team was with him.

'Stand by, stand by! That's Bravo One mobile, left from the yard. Danny has.'

Danny's life with his grandfather had turned full circle. When he had set out to find Fergus more than a year earlier, he had been the target of a surveillance operation by MI6. Now he was part of a special surveillance team himself.

He squeezed the pressel on the gear stick of the silver Mazda he was driving to activate the concealed microphone.

'Danny still has Bravo One held at lights, indicating right. Phil, can you?'

39

The answer came back immediately in Danny's radio earpiece.

'Phil can.'

'Roger that, Phil. Lights to green, Bravo One mobile. That's right at the lights.'

The Land Rover made the right turn but Danny continued straight on. A few moments later the Land Rover passed a junction on the left and Phil turned his green Vauxhall Vectra onto the road, behind Fergus's vehicle.

'Phil has Bravo One.'

Danny was pleased that he'd got the first part of the job right, knowing that it would be his turn to take up the follow again before long. It was a relatively simple job: they had a pretty good idea where Fergus was heading because of previous surveillance work. But it was important to keep eyes on him—for his safety and to see if anyone else was following him. It was also vital, after all the training and practice, for the newly formed team to gain experience of working smoothly together on a real operation.

'That's Bravo One indicating left at the roundabout. Lee, can you?'

Lee was behind the wheel of his blue Ford Mondeo, two cars behind Phil.

'Lee can.'

Danny was already driving back towards a junction where he could comfortably slip in as the following vehicle once again. He knew the road network well. Since moving into an MI5 safe house on the edge of Manchester, one of the team's main jobs had been to familiarize themselves with both the city roads and the Greater Manchester area.

All that had been happening while phase two of

40

the operation was completed. And phase two had gone exactly to plan: Fergus had expertly carried out the very acts of sabotage and vandalism that the twins were now asking him to investigate.

The tooth microphone was working perfectly. Each car had a receiving station concealed under the rear seat, and as Danny took a right turn and came into range, he heard Fergus's voice clearly in his earpiece.

'So, what do the police reckon about these three incidents?'

Will's sarcastic laugh and cynical reply was more distant, but still quite audible. 'The police have been their usual inefficient selves, Mr Watts. They come, they make notes and then they tell us they'll be in touch if there are any developments, which there never are.'

'So you've no idea who might be doing this?'

There was a pause before Will spoke, as though he were racking his brain to work out who might have the nerve to target their company. 'One of the Moss Side gangs, perhaps—there are a lot of them. Trying to muscle in on a legitimate business so they can launder illegally gained money, perhaps.'

'This business of yours . . . If you don't mind me saying, it must have taken quite a lot of cash to set up.'

'Oh, it did, but Mummy helped with the finance, and we're doing tremendously well. It was Teddy's idea, while we were still at uni. We read chemistry, but neither of us liked the thought of being stuck in some laboratory working for someone else. The business makes a lot of money and gives us time for the sort of lifestyle we enjoy.'

41

'And what's that?'

Will laughed. 'We like a good time. Clubs . . . interesting people. We have quite a number of celebrity friends.'

In the Mazda, Danny shook his head as he listened. *Mummy!* He hadn't met the twins yet, but just listening to Will was enough to turn his stomach. All that money and privilege, and all they were interested in doing was messing up people's lives with drugs. If the int was right. And Danny was already thinking that it was.

He dropped a gear and told himself to focus on the job, just like his grandfather always told him, then he heard Fergus's voice again.

'So you've had no contact from anyone? No demands? No threats?'

'No, nothing at all. To be absolutely honest, Mr Watts, we're completely in the dark.'

Danny smiled as he heard the words: phase two had been a total success.

'Lee's held at the lights. Bravo One through and still mobile. Lee does not have.'

Danny reached a junction, saw the Land Rover pass by and then eased the Mazda into the traffic flow. He squeezed the pressel on the gear stick.

'Danny has Bravo One.'

7

Fergus and Danny were sitting opposite Dudley at a table in a motorway services fast food outlet off the M60. It was late, after eleven p.m. At other tables, a few truck drivers sat hunched over newspapers as they stabbed at plates of chips.

Two teenage girls in jeans and padded jackets, both with heavy rucksacks on their backs, wrapped their hands round steaming brews of hot chocolate as they passed their table. One of them glanced at Danny and whispered something to her mate and they both began to giggle.

Dudley, buttoned up in his overcoat as always, heard the laughter and glanced at the girls. He shook his head at the unwanted interruption and then grimaced at the plastic beaker in front of him. It was brimming with thin, brown, lukewarm liquid. He had asked for tea; it didn't even look close, and it certainly wasn't the sort of brew he was accustomed to drinking.

'The twins are clean,' said Fergus. 'Completely. Their flat, their cars, their computers, everything. And it's not down to luck or any normal anti-surveillance procedures. They're taking instructions from someone very experienced. Someone in the know.'

Dudley received the news philosophically, his face giving away nothing as he took in the information. But they all knew that Fergus's words confirmed what Dudley had suspected from the beginning, and that an already tough and dangerous job was likely to get even tougher and more dangerous.

In the short time that Fergus had been 'working' for the Headingham twins, the most advanced and sophisticated technology had been used to try to track down the location of their DMP—without a sniff of success. With access to their home, their business premises and even their computers, Fergus had been in the perfect position to place tracking and surveillance devices.

But nothing had been found, which could only mean that everything was being expertly hidden. It was all *too* clean; the twins even paid their tax bills on time.

Dudley looked at Fergus. 'Are you telling me that someone on our side, someone on the inside, is advising the Headingham twins?'

Fergus shrugged. 'Not necessarily one of ours, but certainly someone trained to the same level as'—he hesitated for a moment and then shrugged again—'as someone like me. We've done the high-tech stuff and the regulation checks—pre-opened their mail before it gets to the sorting office, searched through their rubbish—but there's just nothing at all. They even use pay-as-you-go phones and change the SIM cards every day so their calls can't be traced. And whatever calls they make, they don't make them from home, or from the office. It's just too good. Too professional.'

On the plastic tabletop was a copy of that morning's *Daily Mail*, open at an inside page. The headline made grim reading:

CLUBLAND RIOT
ENDS IN MURDER

Dudley nodded towards the newspaper. 'That's only on an inside page because it was late news and it happened in France. But it's going to get worse. Here and everywhere else.'

The story had made the late editions of most of the daily newspapers and was being heavily featured in the daytime news bulletins. Police in riot gear, some on horseback, had been called in as rioters poured out of a club, smashing shop windows and overturning cars before setting them alight. The newspaper report described the French city centre as becoming 'like a war zone' for more than two hours as police fought to regain control.

For once Dudley's usually placid face showed a flash of anger. 'We know that the man responsible for the killing was on Meltdown. He went completely berserk, and he wasn't the only one. Fortunately the French authorities have managed to keep the Meltdown connection from the press, but it can't continue for much longer. The irresponsible bastards who created this monster of a drug have to be stopped quickly—I've got the Europeans breathing down my neck: they want us to stop Meltdown being manufactured, and immediately.'

He stared down at the newspaper, reading the story again, and Danny took a sip of the Diet Coke he'd been nursing while they waited for Dudley's next words of wisdom.

Danny was getting used to waiting, having discovered for himself that the job wasn't always as exciting as people imagined. He'd spent long days watching and waiting outside the twins' impressive glass-and-steel, canal-view penthouse apartment in Castlefield.

Whenever the twins left the apartment, Danny and the rest of the team had followed in their vehicles. But so far the twins had done nothing more than make occasional trips to the coach yard or late-night visits to Manchester's fashionable restaurants and clubs. It was boring, regulation surveillance work—which Fergus called a 'hurry up and wait' operation, meaning they had to hurry

45

into action and then spend endless hours waiting for something to happen.

But Danny, being Danny, had soon become pissed off with the waiting bit. He complained to his grandfather, desperate to get in on the action and, much to his surprise, had been given the go-ahead. Fergus had moved from the safe house into an expensive hotel once he had started working for the twins, and he was charging them the full whack for his luxury accommodation.

Teddy and Will knew about Danny from the press stories, so when Fergus told them that he needed extra help and was bringing his grandson in, there was no argument.

Danny moved into the hotel too, and for the past two days he'd been checking out the office on the pretext that someone inside the business might be involved in the acts of sabotage and vandalism.

'And you, Danny?' said Dudley, turning to him. 'What about the office?'

Danny shrugged. 'Not a thing. I've been through the phone records, letters, the lot—every piece of paper I could get my hands on. The twins haven't been around but there's always someone keeping an eye on me.'

Dudley frowned at his beaker of tea, considered risking a sip of the tepid liquid, which looked pathetically weak even though the tea bag was still floating on top, but then decided against it. He looked at Fergus again. 'So what do you propose to do next? You didn't bring me to this haven of culinary delight just to buy me a cup of tea.'

Fergus almost smiled. 'I want your go-ahead to take a more proactive line.'

Dudley raised his eyebrows slightly. 'Meaning?'

'The twins suspect that one of the Manchester gangs might be trying to muscle in on their legitimate business.'

'I've read that in your sit reps.'

'Well, I want to bring in one of the gang bosses for real. I'll tell him where the Meltdown is coming from. He's a nasty bastard and if I set him up right, he'll want the business for himself.'

'And what exactly is the point of that?'

'He'll scare the boys shitless. They're all mouth and no trousers. Once they believe that it's their precious Meltdown everyone's after and not their little travel firm, they'll realize they need me even more. I'll get them out of the shit when the gang boss comes looking for the Meltdown and then they'll take me into their confidence.' Fergus sat back in his chair and sighed. 'That's the theory anyway.'

Dudley didn't look completely convinced. 'And is that all?'

'No, not quite,' said Fergus. 'There's a girlfriend; her name's Storm.'

'Storm? *Is* that a name?'

Fergus shrugged.

'And whose girlfriend is she?'

'One of the twins', I'm not sure which one.' Fergus turned and looked at Danny. 'He's gonna get to know her.'

'What d'you mean, get to know her?' said Danny. 'I already do. I was talking to her in the office today.'

'And?'

'Well ... she's ... she's all right. Seems quite nice.'

Fergus shook his head and sighed. 'I'm not

47

interested in knowing if she's nice. I want to find out what she knows. Chat her up a bit; use your charm.'

'Charm? What charm?'

'Get some!' said Fergus firmly. 'Just chat her up.'

Dudley looked over at the two teenage girls, who were still casting the occasional flirtatious glance in Danny's direction. He nodded towards them, causing Danny to look round. One of the girls smiled and beckoned, and Danny quickly turned back, his face aflame with embarrassment.

'I don't think it's me or your grandfather they're smiling at,' said Dudley to Danny. 'They seem to find you . . . interesting and attractive. Perhaps you are—I have no idea about these things—but you'd better make yourself interesting and attractive to this Storm.'

Fergus saw Danny suddenly look anxious. He laughed. 'Don't worry, Danny, you've got the better half of the job. While you're chatting up Storm, I'll be making the acquaintance of Mr Siddie Richards.'

8

There was nothing, absolutely nothing, good about Siddie Richards. He was evil. And proud of it.

Siddie had spent much of the first twenty years of his adult life behind bars, mainly for crimes of extreme violence. But he'd never served time for the most serious crimes he'd committed, because Siddie had literally 'got away with murder'. More than once.

When Siddie reached the age of forty, he finally got wise and decided, reluctantly, to let others carry out the acts of violence for which he was famed and feared. Five years on and Siddie ran one of Manchester's biggest criminal gangs. There was very little that was illegal and lucrative that Siddie wasn't involved in. Gambling, extortion, prostitution, drugs—they were all separate arms of the Siddie Richards business empire.

Siddie was vain and arrogant. He never tired of watching the *Godfather* movies over and over again. He knew every character, every scene and virtually every line, and would quote them endlessly to his minions and to his long-suffering wife, Dawn.

And like his screen hero, Don Corleone, he believed in the old maxim of 'honour among thieves'. It meant that he operated by a simple rule: when he went into business with another criminal, he would never do the dirty on his new partner; not unless they did the dirty on him. If they did, his vengeance was swift, merciless and final. So it didn't happen. Ever.

Fergus had made the appointment to meet the gang boss after a couple of drinking sessions with one of Siddie's henchmen in a pub in the Moss Side area of Manchester. It had been relatively easy. All Fergus had needed to do was make the gangster believe it was possible that he knew the way into the Meltdown drug set-up.

Going by his old alias of 'Frank Wilson', Fergus told his gangland contact that he knew the makers of the drug, who were ripe for a takeover. All it would need was muscle and organization.

The response came back quickly: Siddie was

prepared to meet and talk with 'Frank Wilson'.

The following day Fergus took a taxi out to Cheadle; like the twins, Siddie preferred to conduct his business meetings in the comfort of his home.

The house was worth well over a million; it was located in an area favoured by top footballers and celebrities based in the north-west. Fergus got his taxi driver to drop him off close to the house and then walked the last few hundred metres.

A high wall and an elaborately decorated pair of tall wrought-iron gates protected the property. Fergus pressed the button beneath the voice intercom connected to the house.

The voice that answered through the tinny speaker was surprisingly high-pitched and thin. 'Yes?'

'It's Frank Wilson.'

There was a low clunk as the mechanism was set in motion, then the two heavy gates began to glide open noiselessly.

Fergus walked through and up the drive, past well-kept lawns with large statues of Greek gods and goddesses. The house was mostly mock-Tudor, with thick black beams and heavily leaded windows, but a few other styles appeared to have been thrown in for good measure.

The wide front door of heavy oak stood under a canopy supported by marble columns. As Fergus reached for the large black knocker, the door swung open on huge hinges and he got his first close-up view of Siddie Richards.

He wasn't a pretty sight; he reminded Fergus of a pit-bull, but he was considerably less attractive. Not particularly tall—five nine or ten—broad and barrel-chested, with hardly any neck and a square shaved head. A puckered scar from an old battle ran from just above his right eyebrow down to the bottom of his right ear.

Siddie wasn't going to win any beauty contests, and when he spoke, the high-pitched voice didn't fit the look.

'Mr Wilson,' he said, extending his right hand.

'Frank, please,' answered Fergus as the thick, podgy fingers clasped his own, firmly.

'Call me Siddie. We'll go into my study.'

Fergus followed Siddie along a highly polished parquet floor, past garish reproduction furniture that Siddie usually described as 'Louis the something'.

Standing to one side of the open doorway to the kitchen was a huge guy who looked as though he weighed in at about eighteen stone, most of it muscle. Then, behind him, an even bigger guy appeared: by contrast, this one was pure blubber and he filled the whole doorway. Neither gave any sign that they had noticed Fergus as he sized them up.

'All right, boss?' said Mr Muscles as Siddie passed them.

'Yeah, I'm in a meeting. No interruptions.'

The gang boss led Fergus into a room with floor-to-ceiling bookshelves on two of the walls. They were crammed with neatly arranged red leather-bound books.

Siddie lowered himself into a leather chair behind a large oak desk and gestured for Fergus to sit on the smaller chair in front of him.

'You must be quite a reader,' said Fergus as he settled into the chair.

51

'Never opened one of 'em,' said Siddie, his small eyes weighing up his visitor. 'My Dawn bought 'em from some place where they fit books to the colour scheme. She reckons it gives the place a bit of class, but she don't read either.' He glanced over at a small round table where bottles and full crystal decanters huddled together. 'Drink?'

Fergus shook his head.

'Good,' said Siddie. 'So let's get down to business.'

*　　　*　　　*

What Siddie Richards lacked in good looks, Storm Karlsson possessed in bucketloads. She was beautiful. Five feet six, lithe, ash-blonde, shoulder-length hair, blue eyes and high cheekbones.

Storm was a nineteen-year-old stunner, and she knew it. And like Danny said, she was 'nice'. Pleasant. Sunny. The twins had brought her into the travel business because she was good to have around: she could make even middle-aged, paunchy businessmen believe that they were the answer to every beautiful girl's dream.

When Storm wasn't meeting and greeting for the twins, she spent her working time flitting between their apartment and the office at the coach yard, occasionally answering the phone but mainly, as far as Danny could see, moving sheets of paper from one filing cabinet to another.

Danny was sitting at the office desk, supposedly checking through phone records. He watched Storm slide another sheet of paper into a filing cabinet, looking extremely pleased with herself for successfully completing the operation.

She was wearing a black jacket and skirt, which ended just above the knees. She looked great—maybe a little too smart for the scruffy, untidy office, but Storm was in her PA role so she'd gone for the PA look.

Danny took a deep breath, thinking again about his grandfather's order to 'chat her up a bit'.

He hadn't realized that this was going to be part of the job. Acting. Playing a part. Fergus was doing it with Siddie Richards; now it was up to him to be equally convincing. But then Siddie Richards was an ugly great thug and Storm was a beautiful young woman. Danny took another deep breath and told himself that this was work and to just get on with it.

'You worked here long?'

It wasn't the most original or convincing of chat-up lines but Storm turned from the filing cabinet and flashed him a dazzling smile. She seemed to need to consider the question for a moment before answering. 'About eight months. I think. Time goes so quickly, doesn't it?'

Storm spoke with an accent that was pure Home Counties. And as Danny desperately wondered what gambit he could come up with next to keep the conversation going, he seized on this. 'You're not from round here then?'

Another gem from the book of all-time worst chat-up lines, but it didn't seem to bother Storm.

'I'm not from anywhere, really. My mother was Swedish—she died when I was quite young. My father has always worked abroad—he's always on the move, so I hardly ever see him. Anyway, he sent me to be properly educated at boarding school here in the UK.'

'So are you going to go to university?' Danny asked.

Storm laughed.

'No. I did Textiles and Media Studies at A level. My father would have liked me to have taken more academic subjects and then go to uni. But it's not my thing, and to be honest, I wasn't bright enough.' She smiled. 'Academic stuff is so boring!'

Danny nodded as he thought back to his own schooldays. He'd done OK at GCSEs but life on the run with Fergus meant he'd never got as far as taking A levels.

'I came to Manchester about a year ago,' Storm continued. Danny was in luck: she obviously preferred chatting to shifting paper.

'Why Manchester?'

'A job. It was supposed to be in fashion. You know—buying.' She shrugged her shoulders. 'Actually I was little more than a glorified sales assistant.'

Danny was on a roll, ready with his next question. 'So how did you get this job? I can't see you queuing down the Job Centre.'

Storm smiled into his eyes and perched herself delicately on the corner of the desk.

'No, I met the twins at a nightclub. We got talking and then I . . . well, I started seeing them.'

'*Them?*' said Danny, raising his eyebrows.

'Mmmm,' said Storm thoughtfully as she gazed out of the window at the city skyline. 'The twins do everything together.'

She looked back at Danny, whose eyes were bulging.

'Oh, no,' she said quickly. 'Not that. Well . . . I wouldn't know about that. The three of us are just friends.'

'Oh,' said Danny. 'But I thought you and—'

'Everyone does. And I did at first. I thought I was sort of going out with Teddy, because he was the one I first spoke to. Then I thought maybe I'd got it wrong and it was Will who fancied me.'

'And didn't he?'

'I don't know. The thing is, I'm not sure if the twins have . . .' She paused for a moment. 'The thing is, they're really possessive about me. They hate it if we're in a club and someone comes on to me.'

'And you don't mind? Them being so possessive?'

'Not really. They're like two big brothers. And I like them, I really like them. And I love this job. I get well paid and I don't have to work hard. And I go to all sorts of interesting places.'

She edged a little closer along the desktop towards Danny. Close enough for him to smell the expensive perfume she was wearing. She was looking at him more closely now; differently, as if she were weighing him up, seeing him for the first time.

'What about you?' she said softly. 'Will told me that your granddad is some sort of hero and that you've done really brave things as well.'

Danny shrugged. 'It was just stuff we had to do. I'm not meant to talk about it.'

Storm smiled another of her dazzling smiles. 'You're modest. I like that. The twins show off a lot—it's not nice. And they've got some real morons working for them.'

'Yeah, I've noticed.'

'But you seem—'

Heavy footsteps sounded on the exterior metal

55

stairway that led up to the office, and Storm quickly slid off the desk and moved back to the filing cabinet.

The door swung open and a young guy of around twenty walked in. He was thickset and crop-headed. His face was puffy and pale, with dark rings around the eyes, which took on a staring, almost manic look as they settled on Danny.

'Oh,' said Storm, acknowledging the newcomer, 'you're back at last. Well, you still don't look too good.'

The young man had obviously been expecting to find Storm alone. He stared at Danny. 'Who's he? What's he doing here?'

'This is Danny,' said Storm, concentrating a little too hard on the filing to be completely convincing. 'He's working here.'

'Yeah? Well, no one told me,' he said as he strode over to her. Danny could see that he was standing too close to her for comfort, staring intently at her face.

Storm edged away. 'You haven't been here,' she said, not looking at him. She turned to Danny. 'Danny, this is Albie; he works for the twins too. But he's been ill.'

Danny stood up and nodded at Albie. 'All right?'

Albie ignored him and turned back to Storm. 'I'm all right now. A lot better.' He put his hand on her shoulder. 'I thought we could get a coffee or something, have a talk.'

Storm shrugged off his hand and grabbed a sheet of paper from the top of the filing cabinet. 'I'm really busy, Albie. I'm sorry. Another time maybe.'

Albie moved closer still. Much too close. His face was almost in Storm's as he spoke. 'You can take a

56

break, can't you? You're allowed that. Just come and have a coffee with me.'

As Storm backed away, Danny took a few steps across the office so that he was immediately behind Albie. 'She told you, she's busy. So leave it.'

Albie wheeled round with lightning speed, his eyes burning into Danny's. 'What the fuck has it got to do with you!' he yelled.

Danny took in the clenched fists, the glaring eyes, the beads of perspiration on Albie's forehead. His pulse began to race but his voice was calm. 'Back off,' he said quietly.

For a few seconds it looked as if Albie was going to leap at Danny. But he didn't. His eyes flicked back to Storm, then he wrenched open the door, went out and slammed it shut behind him, and they heard him clatter down the stairway.

Danny looked at Storm and raised his eyebrows. 'Nice guy.'

Storm's lovely face was much paler than usual. Her mouth trembled momentarily, then she took a deep breath and smiled gratefully at Danny.

'He's a creep,' she said. 'And I don't think he's better at all. If anything he's worse than ever. The twins say he's useful but . . .' She paused, came over and gave Danny a kiss on the cheek.

'My hero,' she said warmly. 'Thank you.'

Danny shrugged his shoulders and smiled. 'No problem.' Maybe his chat-up technique wasn't perfect, but Danny reckoned he'd made some progress.

*   *   *

Fergus and Siddie had concluded their business.

It was a simple and straightforward deal. In exchange for providing the 'cast-iron' information that the Headingham twins were the makers and suppliers of Meltdown, 'Frankie' was walking away with five thousand pounds in used twenty-pound notes as a down payment. Once Siddie and his boys had moved in and taken over the operation, Frankie was to receive another fifty grand. Cash. Frankie had given Siddie a mobile number, which he would call when everything was sorted.

That was it. Business done. Frankie had supplied everything Siddie needed to know: a description of the twins, the address of their apartment and details of their regular comings and goings. He couldn't tell him where the drug was being made because he didn't know, but Siddie was more than confident that he could discover that information for himself. He would simply make the twins an offer they couldn't refuse.

The gang boss had listened in silence as Frankie told him in detail about Teddy and Will Headingham, and when he'd finished, Siddie shook his head in disgust. 'Who'd have thought, eh? These privileged kids, they've got everything. Expensive education, university, the lot. And what do they do with it?'

He reached into a drawer of the desk and pulled out a wad of notes held together by a thick elastic band. 'They turn to crime, that's what they do. It's not right. Just shows you the way the world is going, eh, Frankie. It's definitely not right.'

Fergus didn't count the cash that Siddie handed over to him. He knew there was no need.

They walked back to the front door and Siddie held out his hand; this time, when they shook,

Siddie didn't let go at once.

'I'm sure you've heard about the way I do business,' he said quietly, staring into Fergus's eyes. 'This looks like a very lucrative deal for us both. But'—he let the 'but' linger menacingly before continuing—'if this is a scam, or if you're trying to have me over in any way, then I'll come looking for you, Frankie, or whatever your name is, because frankly, *Frankie*, I don't give a shit. And when I find you—and I will—then it won't matter what your fucking name is. Because you'll be dead. *Capisce?*'

9

The clock on the dashboard of Lee's Mondeo flickered as it moved on yet another minute to 8.47 p.m.

Danny sat low in the passenger seat as he pushed forward the on/off switch on the side of the Taser stun gun in his jacket pocket. A Taser would jolt 100,000 watts into a body when jammed against it, and that was enough to instantly drop a small horse.

Danny had got used to handling various longs and shorts during his training, but the Taser felt heavy and unfamiliar in his hand.

Drizzle had been falling for the past hour, dampening the road surfaces and the parked vehicles so that they gleamed in the streetlights. It was a light but constant rain, enough to keep most pedestrians off the streets.

Danny sighed. 'I think she fancies me.'

'Who?

'Storm, the blonde bombshell.'

Lee raised his eyebrows as he thought back to the surveillance photographs he had taken of Storm at the beginning of the operation. He was the one who had come up with the nickname of the 'blonde bombshell'. It fitted her perfectly.

'And what makes you think that?' said Lee, looking at Danny.

'I dunno. The way she looks at me. And smiles.'

'Yeah, I can imagine. But don't get too carried away—you've got a job to do, Danny boy.'

'I know, and I am. I'm just getting to know her, like my granddad said.'

'Listen, Danny,' said Lee, more seriously. 'A word of advice . . .'

'Yeah, I know: never mix business with pleasure. And I'm not going to.'

'Good to hear it,' said Lee. 'Start messing with women when you're on a job and it can mess with your head. Women are clever, you know.'

Danny laughed. 'Oh, so you're the expert on women, are you?'

'Not me, mate. You should talk to Phil—he's been married three times.'

'Yeah?'

Lee nodded. 'Mind you, the last one walked out on him a few years ago, so he obviously hasn't got the hang of it yet, either.'

'How d'you know all this?'

'I've spent a lot of time with Phil since you got your cushy office job. You get to chat up the girlfriend, sit in a warm office shuffling the occasional bit of paper, drinking poncy coffee four times a day and we do the routine surveillance stuff. How fair is that?'

Danny smiled. He was glad to be back at work with Lee. But tonight wasn't routine. Tonight they expected Mr Siddie Richards to pay a visit to the Headingham residence.

It was a Wednesday, and Wednesday night was one of the few occasions when the Headingham twins were regularly apart. They took it in turns to visit their widowed mother. When they were not off on one of their foreign trips, she liked to see them separately, on alternate weeks, so that she could devote herself to one of her beloved sons on his own.

Fergus had tipped off Siddie about the weekly outings and he reckoned that the gang leader would pick that Wednesday to make the home-alone twin an offer he dare not refuse.

Lee peered out through the blurry windscreen, then glanced over at Danny. 'So what you gonna do when this is over?'

Danny shrugged. 'Dunno. Haven't thought about it much.'

'You could come in with us, you know, the Security Service. I might even give you a reference. Or maybe you'd prefer to go over to the dark side and do all that army SAS stuff like Phil and your granddad.'

Danny looked at Lee: he had asked him about his life at MI5, and while Lee hadn't told him much, he got the impression that he loved the work. He started to reply, then glanced up at the street ahead and suddenly broke off to hit the pressel on the Mondeo's gear stick.

'Stand by! Stand by! That's a grey Jaguar, four up, approaching apartment building.

Fergus acknowledge.'

Fergus's voice came back immediately.

'Roger, that.'

'Phil acknowledge.'

Phil was just as quick with his response.

'Roger, that.'

The Jaguar slid to a standstill at the kerbside just past the building as Danny and Lee sank lower into their seats.

Lee was impressed. 'Well done, mate. I'll give you that reference.'

Danny didn't even have time to nod his thanks.

'That's the vehicle static outside the building. Wait . . . wait . . . engine still on, lights on . . . wait . . .'

For a couple of minutes the Jaguar driver kept the engine running.

'No change . . . wait . . .'

Then two doors opened, one front and one rear.

'Stand by, stand by. That's two possible x-rays out of the car. One fat, one just massive. Both black leather on jeans. No sign of x-ray one. Both foxtrot towards apartment building. Engine and lights still on.'

Danny swore silently. He knew that his grandfather needed Siddie Richards himself in the apartment. But he also knew that Fergus wouldn't panic. Fergus never panicked. He improvised.

Danny went back on the net.

'That's two possibles complete in apartment building. What we doing?'

A moment later Fergus's orders came through:

'Phil, move in closer to Jag. Lee and Danny, stay where you are. Listen in for more instructions once I find out what's happening.

62

That's me foxtrot to service entrance at back of building.'

10

Teddy Headingham hardly knew what hit him. One minute he was enjoying the light supper of scrambled eggs and smoked salmon he had prepared for himself; the next he heard a thunderous crashing from the hallway as the locked front door of the apartment crashed open and then two of the most terrifying men he had ever seen came hurtling towards him.

There was no time to move, grab his mobile, shout, or even use the knife and fork in his hands as some sort of defence against the attack. He just sat, frozen, as the first man pulled back his right arm and smashed him in his handsome face, sending him crashing back off the chair and onto the carpeted floor.

Blood spurted from Teddy's busted nose as his uninvited guest straddled his chest and pinned him painfully to the carpet, stopping him from moving. Teddy wasn't thinking about moving anyway; he looked up as Mr Muscles glared into his eyes and breathed on him with foul-smelling tobacco- and booze-tainted breath.

'Don't move, don't shout, don't say a single fucking word till I tell you! You got that?'

Teddy just managed to give a terrified nod as he fought to stop himself choking on the blood that was oozing from his split lips into his throat.

The sheer weight of Mr Muscles' bulk was more

than enough to make certain his victim didn't move an inch. But just to make sure he had his victim's total co-operation, Mr Muscles opened one of his huge fists and slapped Teddy so hard it made his head spin and his eyes water.

Teddy gasped, but he didn't cry out.

Mr Muscles returned the blood that had splashed onto the sleeve of his leather jacket by wiping it clean on Teddy's shirt. He smiled. 'Good boy. Well done. I'm glad we understand each other.'

*   *   *

In a wall socket in a corner of the room, a double plug adaptor that Fergus had installed in the twins' apartment on an earlier visit was picking up every detail of Teddy's torment. Inside it was a minute bug—a microphone and transmitter that had constant power when it was plugged in.

Outside, in the Mondeo, Danny winced as they heard Teddy take the blows.

Lee saw Danny grimace. 'Part of the job, mate—don't let it get to you. Just focus on what we have to do.'

Phil had parked his Vauxhall closer to the apartment and Siddie Richards's Jaguar, ready to go into action the minute he got the order. He nodded as he heard Teddy get another friendly slap; things were getting interesting at last.

Fergus was approaching the service entrance. That afternoon he'd taped back the lock on the door at the rear of the building. As he listened to the one-sided encounter through his earpiece, he hoped that Siddie's heavies hadn't been instructed to kill Teddy if he didn't co-operate fully. He thought it unlikely—they wanted Teddy's information—but with a monster like Siddie Richards, he couldn't be sure.

And Fergus needed Siddie to go into the apartment. He had to give it a while longer.

For the next few minutes they all listened as first one then the other heavy used his own particularly favoured torture technique on Teddy to soften him up. Teddy screamed like he'd never screamed before as he absorbed the pain.

*   *   *

Blubber Man was proving to be less physical than Mr Muscles, but he carried with him specific tools of the trade. He reached into the back pocket of his jeans and pulled out a large pair of pliers. 'That's a nice set of teeth you've got there.' He grinned at Teddy. 'Let's see how you look without the front two.'

'Wait a minute,' said Mr Muscles. 'We go on like this and he'll be dead. And we don't want that. Not yet, anyway.'

He pulled a mobile from his bomber jacket pocket and punched in a number.

A thin voice answered the call. 'Well?'

'He's ready for you.'

Siddie considered for a moment. 'I hope you didn't bust that main door lock. I don't want a break-in reported.'

Mr Muscles sounded almost indignant at the slur on his professionalism. 'No! I did it right—I used the code. You know, the one I gave you.'

Earlier in the day he had also made a visit to the

apartment building and had quickly discovered the four-digit code number for the electronic key pad on the entrance door. It was easy, a technique he'd perfected as a teenager when he used to look over the shoulders of people using cashpoint machines before mugging them for their card.

This time he'd just smiled at a woman as she approached the door, watched her punch in the numbers, followed her into the building and even got into the lift with her. He waited until she selected her floor and then pressed the button for the one below. He nodded a goodbye and then went back to Siddie with the number securely logged in his memory. Mr Muscles was good at remembering numbers.

Siddie seemed satisfied. 'I'm coming in.'

Mr Muscles ended the call and smiled down at Teddy. 'Now it's really gonna hurt.'

*   *   *

Outside the building, a rear door of the Jaguar opened and Siddie Richards stepped out carrying a baseball bat. Siddie had always had a special liking for the weight and feel of a baseball bat as a weapon of mass destruction.

Danny hit the pressel on the gear stick.

'Stand by, stand by! That's engine and lights off. Wait . . . wait . . . That's x-ray out of the Jaguar, approaching apartment building with a baseball bat.'

Fergus was making his way up the concrete service stairs normally used by contractors. He pushed the pressel on the wire dangling from one sleeve of his jacket.

'Phil, you deal with the driver. Danny, Lee, the two x-rays are yours if they come out of the flat. I'm losing this earpiece now—don't want Teddy to see it.'

Fergus pulled the earpiece from his ear and shoved it into a pocket. As he took the stairs three at a time, he slid a silenced Welrod out of his waistband and pushed the safety catch from right to left so that it was ready to fire.

Designed in the Second World War, and looking like a 20cm length of pipe with a pistol grip stuck under it, the Welrod was still the ultimate silence weapon because it had no working parts once the subsonic round was fired: you couldn't even hear the sound of metal scraping against metal.

Siddie used the code to enter the apartment block reception area. Then he took the stairs—the main ones with the thick carpet and modern art on the walls—reasoning that it wasn't a good idea to be seen in the lift with a baseball bat for company.

Meanwhile Phil was already out of his Vauxhall. He took a pack of cigarettes from his pocket and put one between his lips.

He walked casually up to the Jaguar and knocked on the driver's window. As the man behind the wheel turned to look at him, Phil smiled and pointed at the unlit cigarette in his mouth. The driver didn't return the smile; he just turned away.

Phil knocked again, and this time the electric window slid down and the driver glared.

'Piss off.'

Phil looked offended. 'I only want a light, mate.'

'I haven't got a light. Now piss off before I get angry.'

Phil's right hand was in his jacket pocket. Before

the driver had the chance to say another word, Phil whipped it out and jammed the Taser's two steel probes into his victim's shoulder. The driver didn't have a chance to react; he just shuddered uncontrollably as the electricity crackled. Phil gave him a five-second burst of 100,000 watts and he collapsed onto the passenger seat.

Phil opened the door and lifted the unconscious driver back into a sitting position. The Taser was designed to stun, not to kill, being high wattage but low amperage. But to ensure that the driver remained out of action until well after the operation was over, Phil gave him another five-second burst before closing the door and moving away from the Jaguar into the shadows to await further orders.

11

Siddie had reached the top of the building; the long climb up to the penthouse apartment had done nothing to cool his temper, which was always close to boiling point.

Fergus was waiting on the same floor, peering through the crack in the door to the service stairs. He watched the grim-faced Siddie go by and he waited.

By the time Siddie walked into the apartment, his two henchmen had hoisted Teddy up and then leaned his battered body against one of the expensive, but now bloodstained, sofas.

Teddy's face was a bloody mess; it would be some while before Mummy saw her son at his handsome best—if he lived that long.

Siddie looked down at Teddy and then back at the two gorillas. 'Which one is this?'

Mr Muscles and Blubber Man gazed at each other blankly and then back at Siddie. Mr Muscles shrugged his bulging shoulders. 'We didn't ask.'

Siddie sighed. 'Go and wait in the car while I talk to . . .' He turned back to the young man on the floor and raised his eyebrows enquiringly.

The blood-soaked figure on the carpet swallowed a mixture of blood and mucus and managed to gasp out a single word: 'Teddy.'

'Siddie Richards. You might have heard of me.'

The two henchmen were on their way out when Siddie called after them, 'Use the stairs. And leave the paintings where they are.'

*   *   *

This was exactly what Danny and Lee wanted to hear—they had picked up every word Siddie had spoken through the double-socket bug.

As Fergus watched the two heavies head for the main staircase, Danny and Lee were already out of the Mondeo and into the apartment building, also using the service entrance. Moving into the reception area at the front of the building, they pulled Tasers from their pockets before going through the doors to the main stairs.

Lee checked that Danny had a firm grip on the Taser before whispering to him, 'You all right?'

Danny nodded.

'Good. Don't worry, you'll be OK. You take the one on the right. Be sharp. Don't think, just do.'

Danny nodded again, his mouth suddenly dry

and his hands clammy. He knew why Lee was concerned and anxious to reassure him. He was about to take offensive action for the first time; actually attack another person. Until this moment Danny had always been on the receiving end of an attack, only fighting to escape. This time it would be very different.

*   *   *

Siddie was sitting in an armchair close to Teddy, who was still sprawled against the sofa, one hand holding his side. He was sure that at least one of his ribs was broken.

Siddie toyed with the baseball bat as he considered his options. When he spoke, his words terrified Teddy more than all the punches, blows and kicks he had received in the previous fifteen minutes.

'Now, I see it like this,' said Siddie in his high-pitched voice. 'You've got a business that I want. I like the simple life, Teddy, so I'm giving you a choice.'

Teddy groaned; he was convinced now that he was going to die.

'I could make this long and extremely painful for you, Teddy,' said Siddie, standing up and giving the bat a gentle swing to and fro as if preparing to receive a pitch. 'But I can't be bothered with that stuff any more. So this is what I'm gonna do. I'm gonna ask you just once to tell me all I need to know about Meltdown: where you make it, how you sell it, distribute it—everything. Understand me so far, Teddy?'

Teddy nodded, then winced.

'Good. And you're gonna tell me everything. Right? Because if you don't, I'm gonna hit you once with this baseball bat. It will only take one blow to the side of your head. You'll be dead, Teddy. Gone. *Capisce?*'

Teddy swallowed hard and nodded again.

Siddie gave the bat a proper swing, as if he were attempting to hit the ball out of the stadium. 'And when you're dead, I'll just get everything I need from your brother. Time to start talking, Teddy. And remember, you only get one chance.'

Teddy drew in a breath and opened his mouth. But as he watched Siddie's fingers tighten on the baseball bat, his throat convulsed and he choked.

'All right, Teddy, you've had your chance . . .'

Teddy gasped and once again tried to speak, and then his eyes widened as he saw a figure appear through the door from the hall.

Siddie saw his victim's eyes flick to one side and then the tiny glimmer of hope that followed.

He wheeled round, grasping the baseball bat tightly; ready to take on whoever was behind him.

Fergus was less than three metres away, pistol raised and aimed at Siddie's head.

Siddie's narrow eyes registered a moment of total confusion.

A dull thud sounded and he staggered back, blood spurting from the back of his head like a red aerosol spray before his legs gave way and he fell back like a toppling chimney. He thudded to the floor. Both legs twitched for a moment and then were still.

Fergus walked over and stared down at the body. In death, Siddie's eyes were wide open.

At that instant Teddy's bladder finally gave way,

and he pissed himself. He felt shame, terror, relief that he was still alive—and an overwhelming gratitude towards the man who had saved his life.

'You . . . you killed him,' he mumbled as Fergus turned towards him.

Fergus shrugged, hiding his disappointment that he had been forced to act before Teddy had revealed any of the info on Meltdown. He shoved the weapon back into his waistband. 'He won't be missed.'

12

Mr Muscles and Blubber Man were chatting contentedly as they made their way down the stairs. They rarely got the opportunity to pulverize posh boys; it was almost always other low-life like themselves. So when the chance came along, they liked to enjoy themselves and make the most of it. Their only regret was that it had been all too brief; they could happily have done a lot more damage before Siddie took over. Still, it was a job well done.

The staircase was little used; the residents of the apartment block hadn't paid over the odds merely for a canal view. There were two efficient lifts that made climbing stairs an unnecessary inconvenience.

So the two heavies were not expecting to meet anyone as they plodded down. They reached the landing of the third floor, turned and continued down the next flight of stairs.

Danny and Lee were waiting out of sight on the

second floor, immediately after the next turn. Danny's hands were wet with sweat and he was repeatedly wiping his Taser hand on his jeans so that he could keep a firm grip on the weapon.

His face was a mask of concentration as he got the nod from Lee to go. They both held their Tasers in their right hands as they heard the approaching voices getting louder in the stairwell above them. As Danny turned the corner with Lee, he could see the two targets at the top of the stairs. The huge guys' conversation immediately shut down when they caught sight of Danny and Lee and came down towards them.

Lee kept his eyes lowered: he knew the rule— never make eye contact with a target because he will be alert and suspicious. And no matter how hard an attacker tries to disguise it, his eyes will always show intent, or fear, or determination. The target's inner self-defence mechanism will always spot this.

The two pairs closed on each other, but the targets had no intention of giving way to the two young dickheads coming up towards them.

Lee stopped and stood to one side, with the targets about ten steps above, waiting for them to pass before zapping them from behind.

Danny's head was thumping in time with his heart. He could feel his pulse in his neck; he was certain everyone could hear it as he too stopped and waited.

Then Danny made his mistake. He knew he shouldn't have but he couldn't stop himself: his eyes moved upwards towards the two heavies. Maybe he was checking out where he was going to zap his target, maybe he wanted to see what they were thinking, or maybe he was just scared.

But he did it. He fixed his eyes on the target on his side of the stairs. Blubber Man's pupils closed down as he focused on Danny's eyes. And he knew. Danny had given him all the information he needed.

'Oh, shit!'

The rest happened in an instant. Blubber Man launched himself at Danny, and Lee had no option but to move up to take on Mr Muscles before he too had registered what was happening.

Danny didn't even have time to raise his Taser as the mass of fat slammed into him and projected him down the stairs. His head thumped on the last few steps before crashing back onto the landing.

Starbursts flashed in his head and eyes as his brain struggled to recover. His head was telling his legs to move, to get him up and ready to fight, but the message wasn't getting through. All Danny could do was keep a grip on the Taser as Blubber Man hurled himself down onto his body. Every bit of breath was forced from Danny's lungs and he fought for oxygen, kicking and bucking beneath the giant man as a massive hand gripped his neck and two staring, bloodshot eyes blazed into his own.

'Who the fuck are you?'

Danny didn't even attempt to answer. He didn't have the breath. He couldn't move his hand to zap the huge bulk on top of him. All he could do was writhe and twist as Blubber Man's face came closer. He could smell alcohol and tobacco and feel a couple of days' stubble rasp across his skin as the man shouted loudly into his ear.

'Little shit!' Then Blubber Man's free hand was

reaching into the back pocket of his jeans for the pliers.

Danny didn't know if it was his survival instinct or training—it was as though he was on auto mode. He opened his mouth and sank his teeth into Blubber Man's stubbly face. The huge guy growled and Danny felt the skin break as his teeth sank into the flesh and scraped against cheekbone.

Metallic-tasting blood poured from the wound: Blubber Man screamed and pulled himself free, ripping his face from Danny's teeth. He drew back one massive clenched fist, intending to land a punch that would splatter Danny's brains across the floor.

It gave Danny enough room to move his arm and zap Blubber Man in the chest. But the 100,000 watts crackling into his body wasn't enough. Perhaps it was all those protective, insulating layers of fat, or maybe Danny just didn't ram home the Taser into his chest firmly enough. But as he pulled it away, Blubber Man got up and staggered back, looking stunned and bewildered, then growled like a wounded bear and came back at him.

Danny leaped to his feet, adrenalin driving away the pain and fear as he ducked under the giant's flailing arms, brought the Taser up hard into his guts and gave him a long burst. This time the fat man went down, crashing on top of the prone body of Mr Muscles, who was sprawled out on the landing.

Danny suddenly realized that Lee must have managed to down his target too—he had been aware of nothing but his struggle with Blubber Man.

Lee gave Mr Muscles another burst as he hissed at Danny, 'Give him some more! Keep him down!'

Danny gave the fat man another five seconds and then staggered back against the wall, sucking in air. He became aware of something in his mouth and almost gagged as he spat out a piece of Blubber Man's flesh. He leaned against the wall, gasping, fighting back the vomit that was rising in his throat.

Lee grabbed Danny's shoulders and pulled him upright. He knew exactly what he was going through; everyone has a first time.

He stared into Danny's eyes. 'You'll dream about it for a while but you just have to deal with it. OK?'

Danny took two deep breaths and then nodded. 'Yeah.'

'You did good, mate. Well done. Now clean yourself up.'

13

Danny nodded at his grandfather as he entered the apartment, confirming that Siddie's three thugs had been dealt with successfully. Teddy had managed to haul himself up onto one of the bloodstained sofas and was sitting clutching his damaged ribs with one hand and dabbing his bloodied nose and mouth with pieces of tissue with the other.

Danny's face was still red as the blood pumped around his body. He thought he'd wiped his face clean but there was still a little blood on his neck.

Fergus pointed towards it. 'Yours? You OK?'

Danny wiped his neck and shook his head. 'Theirs. I'm OK.'

But Fergus wasn't convinced. 'Bit of a drama down there?'

'I'll deal with it,' said Danny firmly.

Then he caught sight of the prone body of Siddie; his face had shattered where the bullet entered, and for an instant Danny had an image of Elena, lying dead on the ground in Central Park. He forced the thought away—he couldn't allow himself to dwell on it; it was too painful. He had to focus on the job; concentrate; stay professional.

Instead, he watched his grandfather. Fergus had his own game plan completely worked out. He'd given Teddy long enough to take in the enormity of what had happened in his apartment. Teddy was deliberately not looking at Siddie's body, which lay like a beached whale on the carpet, the blood soaking into the weave. Violence was something he could ask of others; he couldn't cope with it himself.

Fergus sat down next to him on the sofa. Now it was time to get the information he wanted.

'All right. As I've just saved your life, I think it's time I knew exactly what's going on, don't you, Teddy?' He nodded towards the body on the floor. 'And don't give me any crap about him wanting to take over your coach firm. Blokes like that aren't interested in executive travel.'

Teddy hesitated, dabbing at his nose again as he tried to think what to say. 'I . . . I don't know. I honestly don't. I can't imagine why someone like that—'

'Forget it.' Fergus was on his feet. 'Listen, Teddy, you're not paying me nearly enough to get

77

involved in something like this. Consider our contract terminated. Come on, Danny.'

They headed for the door.

'Wait! Please!' Teddy couldn't stop himself from taking another look at Siddie's body.

Fergus stopped, looked back and waited for Teddy to continue.

'What do I do? About . . . that?'

Fergus didn't reply immediately. He was playing a part, appearing to consider whether or not he would help Teddy. It was all an act, and Danny knew it. But his grandfather was good at acting; he knew that too.

'I'll tell you what I'll do, Teddy,' Fergus said at last. 'As a gesture of goodwill. I'll get rid of it for you.'

'You . . . you can do that? But . . . but how?'

'You don't need to know. It'll be done, that's all.'

It would be simple. All Fergus needed to do was put in a call to Dudley and a team of 'cleaners' would come in, remove the body and dispose of it before clearing up the blood in the flat and on the stairs. By midnight the only sign that there had been any sort of disturbance in the apartment would be the smashed-in door. But that didn't matter: it was the top-floor penthouse so no one was going to see it.

'You'd better get yourself down the hospital,' said Fergus to Teddy. 'Check out that damage to your ribs. And by the look of it, you've got a busted nose as well.'

'But what do I tell them? They'll want to know how it happened.'

'Say you were mugged.' It was almost as if he was talking to a child. 'But don't get the police involved. And call your brother. Tell him not to come back here tonight.'

Fergus feigned indifference as he walked over to Siddie's body, but it was a deliberate move; it meant that Teddy couldn't avoid seeing the body yet again as they spoke. Teddy tried not to look down, but then Fergus kneeled to take a closer look at his handiwork.

'Tell your brother to meet you at the hospital and then go to a hotel. By the time you get back here tomorrow the body will be gone. And so will we.'

Teddy struggled to his feet, gasping as a new wave of pain shot through his body. 'Look, there *is* something more . . .'

Fergus had Teddy exactly where he wanted him; all he needed to do now was reel him in. 'Not interested. I'll call you about where to send the rest of my fee. Whatever's going on here is not our problem any more, mate. It's yours.'

Teddy almost gagged as he spoke—he couldn't help glancing down at Siddie's face, the eyes glazed over now like those of a dead fish. 'I want to tell you about it, I want you to stay involved, but I have to speak to my brother first. I have to convince him that it's the right thing to do. We're partners in this. And . . . and it's . . . what we do . . . it's not exactly . . . legal.'

Fergus stood up before replying, looking Teddy straight in the eye. 'You really think I expected legal?' He glanced down at Siddie. 'Illegal doesn't worry me as long as it's lucrative. Very lucrative. But you'd better be quick, Teddy. We've got plenty of other clients waiting out there. You want Danny to drive you to the hospital?'

Teddy shook his head. 'I'll manage.' He looked

79

over at Danny. 'Perhaps you could help me to my car though?'

'Yeah. No problem.'

'Use the stairs, not the lift,' said Fergus to Danny. 'Best not to let anyone see him in that condition.' He saw his grandson's raised eyebrows and nodded.

Danny helped Teddy up and they started to make their way towards the door, but then Teddy stopped, turned, wincing with pain, and looked at Fergus. 'The other two . . . they might still . . .'

'You don't have to worry about them. Danny's taken care of them.'

Teddy stared at Danny, then at Fergus, and then back at Danny as he struggled to take in what they had done that night.

Danny just nodded and smiled and supported Teddy as he shuffled slowly out of the apartment.

As soon as they had gone, Fergus pulled out his mobile and speed-dialled Lee's number. 'Are they still out?'

'Sleeping like babies.'

'Give them another burst and then clear out. Danny's on the way down with Teddy. I want him to see exactly what we've done for him.'

*   *   *

Teddy spotted the two sprawled-out bodies the moment Danny eased him around the turn at the landing above.

He froze. 'Are they . . . are they dead?'

Danny shook his head. 'Stunned. They'll be out for quite a while.'

'But when they do come round . . . they might—'

80

'They'll get out, Teddy, that's what they'll do. And they won't come back.'

They moved slowly down the stairs. When they reached the landing, Teddy stopped by the two bodies.

Mr Muscles was snoring beneath Blubber Man, who still had blood oozing from his face.

Teddy's own face contorted in anger. He leaned on Danny and then viciously kicked Blubber Man in the guts.

'Bastards!'

Blubber Man didn't even stir, and Teddy was ready to get in a few more kicks, but Danny pulled him away.

'Steady on. A few more of those might just wake them,' he told him. 'Let's get you to hospital.'

14

The atmosphere in the office at the coach yard was thick with tension. Will had never before even considered challenging his brother's unspoken leadership and authority. But seeing Teddy's bruised and battered face, and the way he kept flinching as he got another jolt from his cracked ribs, somehow made him seem vulnerable and a little pathetic.

And Will was determined to take advantage of his brother's sudden vulnerability.

'Why should we bring in Watts? He's done his job; he's got rid of the threat. We can pay him off and let him go.'

Teddy was on the defensive, but he'd made up

his mind on what he wanted, telling his brother he'd decided to bring Fergus in on 'all aspects of the business' so that he could oversee their complete security and protection.

'We don't know that what happened last night was anything to do with the attacks here,' he said. 'They might be totally unconnected.'

'So there are more people out there who know about Meltdown? Is that what you're saying? So who's telling them?'

'I don't *know*!' Teddy flinched as a stab of pain shot through his ribs. 'Maybe a dealer has got word on us; maybe it's one of our own. I don't know, Will. All I do know is that I want to bring Watts in. We don't need to tell him everything, just enough. And we'll test him out before we say anything.'

'It's a crazy idea, a total non-starter. We've got our own team,' insisted Will. 'They've always looked after us well enough. What happened in the apartment was a one-off; we're safe now.'

'Our team?' said Teddy. 'Albie? And the rest of them? They were OK when we got going but you know Albie's become a liability.' He paused. The medical staff at the A&E department had patched up Teddy's physical wounds, but the image of Siddie Richards with a bullet hole in his face would not fade from his mind. 'Look,' he said, failing to conceal his impatience. 'We're going to need someone like Fergus.'

Will's face was flushed with anger. 'And how do you know you can trust him?'

'Because he killed someone for me last night! He committed murder to keep me alive! Isn't that enough?' Teddy shifted in his chair to ease the pain from his ribs. 'Watts will do whatever we ask

82

of him as long as the money's right. He said as much last night. That's all he's interested in.'

Will was still glaring at him, obviously intent on saying a lot more.

Teddy levered himself to his feet and crossed the room to where his brother was standing.

'Will, you weren't there! I nearly died!'

*   *   *

Danny drove into the yard and parked up. As he got out of the silver Mazda, he saw Storm standing by the stairs to the office. She was frowning but still looked stunning in a designer suit and high-heeled boots.

'If you've come to look at the computers again, you'll have to wait.' She smiled and then glanced up towards the office. 'They're arguing. I don't know exactly what the problem is, but Teddy's in a terrible state—he's in such pain, and his face looks terrible. Whatever happened to him must have been awful.'

Danny closed the car door as he considered his answer. 'He's just not used to trouble. It's probably not as bad as it looks.'

'But what happened? They said you were there.'

Danny wasn't giving away a thing. 'What did they tell you?'

Storm shrugged. 'There was this guy—some sort of gangster—who was trying to take over the travel business. He beat up Teddy but then your granddad came in and scared him off.'

'That's about it,' said Danny. 'He won't be back, anyway.'

'Then why is Teddy still so scared?'

'I don't know, Storm. You'd better ask him.'

He could see that Storm was puzzled by his evasion. She stared into his eyes, and frowned, searching for the truth.

He returned the look, realizing as he did so that he was quickly becoming as accomplished as his grandfather at telling lies. It went with the territory.

Storm's searching look suddenly turned into one of her most dazzling smiles and her brow cleared. 'Would you like a cappuccino? The twins want me out of the way for a while and it'd be nice to have some company. There's a place down the road that's good. We can walk.'

Danny smiled. 'Yeah, why not.'

As they walked towards the gates, they heard a shout from the workshops.

'Storm!'

They looked back and saw Albie standing in the open doorway.

'Oh, what does he want now?' whispered Storm as he came striding over. She moved closer to Danny, almost as though she was silently looking for his protection.

When he reached them, Albie glared briefly at Danny and then focused on Storm, forcing a smile. 'You all right?'

'Fine, thanks, Albie. You?' Storm's voice quavered a little.

Albie nodded but said nothing more. He just kept smiling at her. The silence went on and on, but Albie had obviously run out of conversation. He just stared at Storm with barely disguised adoration.

Storm glanced at Danny and then turned to head

towards the gates again. 'Bye then, Albie.'

'Where you going?'

'We're, er . . . we're going for a quick coffee.'

'I'll come. I'm not doing anything.'

Danny could almost see Storm searching for a plausible excuse to get rid of Albie. But when it came, it sounded pretty lame and a very obvious put-down. 'We . . . we have to talk about business, Albie.'

'What about later then?' insisted Albie. 'Late. When I finish work. A drink? Or a club maybe?'

Storm smiled. 'Another time, eh?'

*   *   *

Albie watched them until they had passed through the gates, his eyes burning into Danny's back. Then he walked slowly back towards the workshop.

Inside, two of the guys who doubled as security and general workers around the yard were leaning against one of the newly cleaned coaches.

They instantly recognized the look on Albie's face. They'd seen it before and they knew better than to say anything as he passed them. They watched him head across to a greasy metal workbench and pick up a large monkey wrench.

He held it in his right hand and hit it against the open palm of his left hand a couple of times. Then his eyes flashed and he raised the monkey wrench above his head and smashed it down on the workbench. The bench crashed to the ground, the legs collapsing under the vicious blow as nuts and bolts and tools went flying like shrapnel in every direction.

85

Albie dropped the monkey wrench on the concrete, then turned and glared at the two guys, his eyes daring them to make a comment.

*   *   *

The argument in the office was still raging and Will was giving as good as he got. But there was more than twenty years of history between them to overcome.

Teddy was the older brother by a full twelve minutes. He'd always made the major decisions and Will had gone along with them. It worked that way. It was easier. But not this time.

'I don't like it, Teddy. We've only known the guy a couple of weeks and you want to tell him everything.'

'But I don't. Just enough. Look, Will, we've got to face it—if Siddie Richards managed to find out about us, then there's a bloody good chance one of the other gangs might show up before too long. If that happens, I want Watts around.'

'But we've been so careful with security. We've done everything we've been told.'

'Maybe we let something slip. Or someone did. Maybe we're coming to the end of it, Will. We've had a great run. Maybe we need to start thinking about winding it up and moving on.'

'That won't be popular. You know the instructions.'

Teddy sat up in his chair. 'It's *our* business. We can do what we want.' He looked closely at his brother. 'Now, are you with me on this, Will? Just trust me, like you always have done.'

Will hesitated for a moment but then sighed and

nodded. 'But I don't like it, Teddy. I really don't like it.'

Teddy smiled. 'We'll talk to Watts together. Then we'll decide on whether or not he joins us on the Barcelona trip.'

'You mean, you'll decide.'

'*We'll* decide, Will.' Teddy opened a drawer in the desk and took out a pay-as-you-go mobile phone. 'And now we'd better start organizing tonight's production meet.'

15

Doug was the no-questions-asked variety of truck driver, wheels and wagon for hire. He was bowling along the M60, sticking to the speed limit and driving carefully, as country rock blared from the cab's speakers. The traffic was unusually light and Doug was smiling, thinking of the wad of cash he'd pocket for this job.

It was all going like clockwork, as it always did. He'd picked up packages from three different supply depots, then stopped as instructed at the Birch service station on the M62 to collect his passenger.

He was there in the trailer park, sitting reading *Motor Cycle News* on a worn patch of grass by the bins, wearing scruffy jeans, a baggy puffa jacket and a striped scarf, iPod ear-buds in place, a rucksack at his feet. As Doug pulled in, he stood up, folded his paper and pulled on a pair of thin gloves.

The articulated truck's hydraulic brakes hissed as

Doug drew the vehicle to a standstill and then jumped from the cab to open the rear doors. Within a couple of minutes the skinny young guy was in the back of the truck and Doug was pulling back out onto the motorway, heading for the M60. Where possible, he would stick to motorways to keep the ride smooth. Today it was easy. It was going to be the M60 almost all the way.

Doug had no idea that the young guy he'd just picked up was a highly qualified chemist who was supplementing his meagre research assistant's pay carrying out the first half of the Meltdown process in the mobile laboratory in the back of the truck. But he only had the first part of the formula.

The whole operation was based on the way the wartime French Resistance movement operated; the way terrorist organizations still operate today. No one but the twins knew the whole story. Everyone else, from the chemists, through to drivers, loaders and security guys, only knew just what they needed to know when they needed to know it. It was brilliant. By keeping the process in two parts and mainly mobile, even if someone did blab about the location of the meet, by the time the police or security forces arrived, the DMP would be long gone.

*   *   *

Eventually, Doug arrived back at the Birch services, dropped his passenger off, sent a coded text message and received a postcode and a hangar number in return. For the second time that day he pulled out onto the motorway and headed for the M60.

The production meet was at a decommissioned airfield about an hour north of Manchester. During the Second World War it had been the base for an RAF bomber squadron, but its glory days were long gone.

All that remained of the runways was cracked and broken stretches of concrete, with grass and weeds growing from wide, ugly fissures. The old hangars had been supplemented by newer factory units, creating a ramshackle industrial estate. It wasn't pretty and it wasn't purpose-built, but it was perfectly functional.

The twins had taken a short lease on one of the hangars. The location was good. Ten or more other organizations used the neighbouring units. A vehicle-hire company garaged and maintained its fleet of vans in one; an electrical supplies company used another for storage. Even the police had a presence on the site: the unit next door but one was used by the force as a dog-training centre.

Businesses came and went on a regular basis; there was frequent traffic in and out of the site and no one asked questions. It was that kind of place.

Doug backed his artic into the hangar, watching carefully in his wing mirrors for the signals from the pale and puffy-faced young guy with dark shadows under his eyes who always seemed to be in charge at the meet. There was a shout and his hand came up to signal a stop.

Doug applied the parking brake and switched off. He knew he had backed up to the open tail of another artic. He knew from the sounds that the back of his trailer was being opened and people were getting in. To one side, he could see two sleek black luxury coaches parked up, but he'd decided long ago that if this was dodgy stuff, he didn't want to know about it. Just as long as he got paid, he was happy to sit in his cab, read his paper and listen to his music until he was told to go. *Hear no evil, see no evil* was his philosophy.

16

Teddy had watched the coaches pull out of the yard on their way to the meet, before he asked Fergus if he'd heard of Meltdown. Fergus shook his head.

'It's a drug, a chemical drug. A bit like Ecstasy, but much better.'

'Yeah, I reckoned this was about drugs.'

'Do you have a problem with drugs?'

Fergus smiled. 'I've had a lot of problems with drugs over the years. Specially in Colombia.'

'I mean morally. Do you have a moral objection to drugs?'

Fergus had mentally prepared for this conversation, knowing which way it was likely to go. 'Morality is something you leave behind when you do my sort of work. You just get on with the job. If you stopped to think about what's right and what's wrong, you'd never do it.'

Will couldn't stop himself from interrupting. 'But you were in Colombia trying to bust the drugs cartels—we've read the stories.'

'I was a soldier. I did what I was told.'

'But then a better offer came along?'

'That's right. I spent half a lifetime doing the heroic Queen and country stuff. And for what?

Piss-poor pay and a medal to shove in the back of a cupboard and forget about. FARC offered me a lot of money and I grabbed it. And when I got caught, I didn't have anyone to blame but myself.'

'So money is what motivates you now?' said Will.

'Totally.' Fergus smiled. 'For some reason they took away my army pension.'

Will wasn't smiling. He was the one who still needed convincing; he hadn't been through the Siddie Richards experience. 'And this last job, the suicide bombings. Why you? Why did they pick you when they knew you were a traitor?'

This was the test. Fergus knew his answer had to be believable, and like all the best lies it had to be based on truth. 'MI5 had tracked me down—me and Danny and his friend Elena. The guy behind the bombings was targeting teenagers, grooming them on the Internet, and Elena was brilliant with computers and the Internet, even better than Danny. My speciality is explosives, so they gave us a choice, work for them or'—he lifted his right hand, made a pistol shape and held it against his temple—'goodnight.'

Will still wasn't smiling. 'But why not just use their own people?'

Fergus was calculating his physical responses as carefully as his words, and now was the moment to act as though he was getting bored and irritated with the questioning. 'You think the security services only work with the good guys? That's bollocks. They'll work with whoever can get results. And the best thing for them, with us, was that if it all went wrong, they could deny any knowledge of our involvement.'

'And this . . . . Elena—what happened to her?'

'She's dead. There was a complete fuck-up and she got shot.' Fergus looked at Teddy. 'Just like your friend from last night.' He turned back to Will. 'But they didn't tell you that bit in the papers. And you'll understand why neither Danny nor I have any particular love for the security services or the British government.'

Fergus pushed away his chair and stood up. It was time for the big gamble, the walkout. If it went wrong, there would be no coming back. 'Look, I don't need this. You boys just go play with your Meltdown, or whatever it is you call the stuff.'

He headed for the door of the office, opened it and took a step outside, thinking that maybe he had blown it, when he heard Teddy's voice.

'Mr Watts!'

Fergus stopped and turned back. He stood in the doorway and watched as the brothers exchanged a nod before Teddy spoke.

'We make Meltdown and sell the tablets here and in Europe. We're prepared to show you how we export the tablets but not how or where they are manufactured. Only *we* know the complete formula—no one else has access to that information—and we would like you to be responsible for our personal security in the immediate future; I don't want to risk another Siddie Richards situation. You'll be paid very, very well. Does that appeal?'

Both twins watched Fergus closely as he considered his reply. 'Yeah, the money appeals, but I have to consider our security—mine and Danny's. The places where you make this stuff— are they safe? You get busted and it wouldn't be good to be around.'

92

Teddy glanced at Will, who nodded his agreement for big brother to continue. 'It's been working perfectly for months and it's quite safe. That's all you need to know.'

Fergus nodded slowly; he wasn't going to push it—he'd made the breakthrough. 'I'll look after you, and your happy pills. As long as the price is right.'

'Oh, it will be,' said Teddy, looking hugely relieved. 'And we'd like you to join us on our next trip. To Barcelona.'

Fergus nodded again. 'When's that?'

'Tomorrow.'

17

Albie was forcing himself to concentrate as he prowled around the hangar. It wasn't easy: his brain wasn't functioning properly; he couldn't stop the rage building every time his thoughts turned to Storm walking out of the yard with that cocky little wanker, Danny.

It didn't worry him at all when he saw Storm with Teddy or Will. They were poofs anyway, even if they didn't know it.

Albie knew it. Everyone knew it. They just didn't mention it.

But now Albie had to concentrate. Hard. His job was to oversee the final phase of the Meltdown operation. He never saw the first part. All he knew was that a truck would arrive with the first stage completed. The second stage took place in the other truck and then the pills were ready for

93

transfer into the coaches. He had to make sure that it all went smoothly and that the drugs were stowed properly in the ingenious hiding places on the coaches.

A three-inch-deep cavern extending across the entire floor area of each coach was removed in sections. More tablets would be stashed in hollowed-out blocks of the overhead storage lockers, in the steel legs of tables, in wall panels— anywhere there was a space that could be filled, even in the plush seating. The customers had no idea that they rode to Europe on Meltdown.

If anyone local asked what they were doing, the cover story was that the coaches were being prepared for a round-trip to a top European football match—checked for any minor faults, cleaned, loaded with fresh supplies of excellent food and drink, and generally made ready for the guests paying megabucks for their expensive excursion. All of which was true. The cleaners and local delivery vans arrived during the day to do the legit work and the drugs were stowed when they were long gone.

The twins were proud of the beautifully simple operation they had devised and developed.

And they relied on Albie to see that it all ran smoothly. He'd got the first-stage truck away OK—that driver never caused any bother. But now Albie was struggling.

The trouble was, Freddie Lucas was winding him up something rotten. Freddie was the second-stage chemist, and as far as Albie was concerned, he should have been minding his own business. But he wasn't.

The tablets had emerged from Freddie's truck, each stamped on both sides with its distinctive

'M'—only visible under black light—before being sealed in protective silver foil and then bagged in polythene in batches of fifty.

Now Freddie was watching the lads loading the pills, constantly telling them to be careful, getting in everyone's face, especially Albie's.

The lads had nicknamed Freddie 'Fiery Fred', and it wasn't only because of his mop of flaming red hair. He watched over his Meltdown like a mother hen protecting her chicks, guarding each tablet as if it were a newly hatched egg. And if a bag of pills was dropped or split or even dirtied, he would fly into a rage.

It was obvious that Freddie didn't like Albie. Albie didn't give a toss about that—no one liked him, but if they were wise, they kept out of his way. Freddie wasn't and he didn't.

Albie reckoned that Freddie was just another public school prat; the type that thought that they were better than everyone else, that they knew best all the time, that people like Albie were beneath them.

Albie didn't care about that either, but he was just longing to put his fist into Freddie's smug face. He knew he couldn't—he was already in enough trouble with the twins for previous violent outbursts and his dependence on M. He'd managed to convince them he was over that now, but if Freddie got on his case much more, Albie feared he wouldn't be able to stop himself from laying him out.

There was a nagging ache in Albie's back—maybe it was his kidneys—and a stabbing pain in his chest. Neither would go away, and on top of that it felt as though his head was going to explode.

He was sweating under the arc lights; he needed some more Ms. They always made him feel better. For a while. If only Freddie would piss off, he'd be able to do what he always did and slip a pack into his pocket. That way, he'd have enough for himself and plenty to sell on in one of the clubs. But Freddie wouldn't piss off. And Albie had to be so careful. If he got caught stealing the stuff, he'd be in the shit big time. But he didn't have a choice. He needed it.

He also needed some air. He opened the metal door at the rear of the hangar. The arc lights speared through the doorway and out into the darkness, sparking up what sounded like a pack of wolves.

It was the police dogs; some of them must have been on a sleepover instead of spending a quiet night in front of the fire with their handlers.

A voice shouted, 'Quiet, Bruno! And you, Sasha!'

'Shit,' breathed Albie, pulling the door shut. The last thing they needed was Plod calling round for a late-night chat.

He turned back and looked at the coaches. One of them was already loaded with its cargo of Meltdown; the other was well on the way, and Albie had not had one opportunity to grab a bag.

He went across to the coach that was ready to go. After all, it was his job to check that everything was in order.

Inside, it looked immaculate, more like the interior of a presidential jet than a coach. There were just twenty plush, airline-style seats; the remainder of the interior was filled with stylish high-tech business and relaxation areas—an Internet hot zone, plasma TV screens, DVD players—everything the guests needed to relax or keep tabs on important business was no more than an arm's length away.

Albie shrugged. It looked fine, as always. He went to check the other coach. The false floors had been replaced, as had the overhead locker panels; there was little more to be done—just the bags that would be crammed into the seats. They were always done last. The two loaders were taking a fag break. Albie walked up the gangway, briefly alone on the coach. Now was his chance.

Then he heard someone coming up the steps at the front of the coach, followed by Freddie's grating voice. 'What are you doing, Albie?'

Albie turned round, his eyes boring into the chemist. 'What the fuck has it got to do with you?'

Freddie stood his ground. If he was intimidated, it didn't show. 'I'm responsible for the consignment. I have to know it's been loaded correctly.'

'You! Your job is to make the stuff. It's down to me to check it and load it. Now get out of my face before I stick one of your test tubes up your ginger arse!'

Freddie hesitated. His own temper was of the specifically verbal variety; he didn't go in for violence and he didn't have a death wish. And he knew that Albie was more than capable of carrying out his threat. He backed away. 'I shall speak to the twins about this,' he told Albie.

'Talk to who you like!' Albie grinned as he watched Fiery Fred hurrying away, his flames well and truly extinguished.

'Wanker,' he breathed as he grabbed a bag of Meltdown and shoved it into his jacket pocket.

18

Thnx 4 coffee.
Want 2 do a
club bit ltr?
xx

Danny was with Lee when the text from Storm arrived. They were grabbing a meal in a pizza restaurant just round the corner from Fergus and Danny's hotel.

Phil had the trigger on the twins, who had moved into the Malmaison Hotel in the city centre while their apartment was being sorted.

Danny handed his mobile to Lee, who read the text and then checked his watch. It was 9.45. He handed the mobile back to Danny.

'You going?'

'Dunno. What d'you reckon?'

'I'm not your dad, Danny. You don't need to ask my permission. But if you *are* thinking of going, you should talk to Fergus—and not because he's your granddad, but because he's your boss. The blonde bombshell's not just some good-looking bird, she's a target.'

Danny nodded. Sometimes the fact that Fergus was his grandfather as well as his boss made him uncomfortable when he was with Lee and Phil. It was a bit like a football manager playing his own son in a team; other people might not be convinced he was really there on merit.

But Fergus made a point of never showing Danny any special favours; if anything, he was even tougher on him, but Danny had never been certain how Lee and Phil felt about it.

'Are you OK with the granddad thing? Him and me working together on this, I mean?' he asked Lee.

Lee smiled. 'Listen, Danny. Dudley wouldn't have wanted you if he didn't think you had a part to play. And from what I've seen of Fergus, he wouldn't have agreed to you being in unless you could do a job. That's good enough for me.'

'What about Phil—what does he think?'

'Phil keeps himself to himself, like Fergus, but if he wasn't happy about it all, he'd let Fergus know soon enough. Some day his life could depend on you.' He looked at Danny closely. 'And so could mine.'

Danny finished his pizza, thinking about what Lee had said. He pushed away his plate. He wanted to see Storm away from the office again. He'd enjoyed being with her in the coffee shop; for a short while he'd let himself relax and be normal for once. They got on well and Danny liked the way Storm seemed to be so impressed by the action-packed life she assumed he lived.

He brought himself back to the present. 'Well, I suppose I'll have to go clubbing then. All in the line of duty, of course.'

'Just make sure it is.' Lee laughed through a mouthful of pizza. 'And call your—'

But Danny was already punching in the number on his mobile. He told his grandfather about Storm's text.

'I didn't learn much this morning. She may not know a lot but I reckon it would be a good idea if I met her, don't you?' he asked him.

Fergus couldn't hold back his laugh. 'I'm sure it would. Seems you do have some charm after all. But you're working, Danny, remember that. We need to find that DMP. Keep focused. Tell Lee I want him to back you—you might well meet people who are worth following. We've got to make the most of these opportunities when they come up.'

'Right.'

'And before you meet Storm, give Phil a call. Make sure he knows what's going on. And be careful.'

'Right,' said Danny again. He hung up, thinking that his date with Storm had already turned into much more than a date. Quickly he passed on his grandfather's orders.

'Yeah, thought as much,' said Lee, wiping pizza crumbs from his mouth. 'Why is it that you always get the girl and I get the surveillance?'

Danny grinned. 'Must be my good looks.'

'Something like that.' Lee smiled, then took out some cash and beckoned to a waiter. 'Call Storm, tell her you're up for it. And then you'd better smarten yourself up. Don't want to disappoint the lady, do you?'

*   *   *

Phil was sitting at a small table in the bar of the Malmaison Hotel, holding his mobile to his ear. He couldn't help smiling to himself as he listened to Danny telling him the score.

'So you did make sure you flossed, eh?'

'Yeah, yeah, yeah.'

Danny closed down and Phil put his mobile away.

100

At the tables all around him, people were chatting and laughing as wall speakers pushed out soft lounge-lizard music. Phil thought back to the bars in what was left of the best hotels in Baghdad, where the background music had been a cacophony of helicopters whirring overhead, machine-gun fire and exploding shells, some of them close enough to make the building shudder.

Phil checked his watch: it was nearly 11.20. He glanced up and saw Teddy coming down the carpeted, sloping entrance to the bar, closely followed by his younger brother. Teddy was moving slowly and awkwardly—he was obviously still in a lot of discomfort and wore sunglasses to hide the embarrassment of his black eyes.

Phil sat back in his chair and watched him find a space at a padded, high-backed banquette on the far side of the room while Will went to the bar and ordered drinks. He returned to his brother with what Phil reckoned were two glasses of Coke, but before either of them could take a drink, another young guy with a shock of flaming red hair came hurrying into the bar. He didn't look happy.

He spotted the twins, went straight over to their table and sat down. He was too far away for Phil to hear exactly what was being said, but it was quite clear that something was wrong. The twins listened as the guy talked animatedly, occasionally glancing at each other and frowning.

Phil pulled his mobile from the inside pocket of his jacket and pressed the speed dial: the angry red-haired guy was a total newcomer on the scene; this could be an interesting development.

Fergus answered the call immediately. 'What you got?'

19

Storm and Danny were laughing as they hurried towards the club, avoiding the puddles and pretending to dodge the raindrops like a couple of kids.

As they neared the long queue, Danny realized that he hadn't really laughed for months. He thought of Elena, and for a moment he felt guilty, as if he shouldn't be here enjoying himself. But he shook the thought away. He was on a job; it was OK. Elena would have told him that.

Instead of joining the back of the queue, Storm made her way up towards the door, grabbing Danny's hand and dragging him with her.

'But don't we have to—?'

'No, Danny, we don't.'

Two black-suited, burly bouncers stood in the doorway. They smiled at Storm, gave Danny a quick, appraising once-over and moved aside so that they could pass straight through. As they headed into the club, Danny spotted Lee, just two back in the queue. He didn't know if Lee had seen him, but even if he had, there would have been no eye-to-eye.

As soon as they stepped into the darkened reception area, staff came hurrying up, as though visiting royalty had arrived. Someone took Storm's coat and the manager came out to welcome her like a long-lost sister, kissing her on both cheeks and telling her how wonderful it was to see her again.

There was no question of them paying to get in.

They were led into the club itself and then told to have a wonderful evening—there was plenty of room in the VIP area.

The pounding, thudding music was so loud that Danny had to shout to be heard. 'What was all that about?'

'What?' shouted Storm.

Danny pointed back to the entrance. 'The special treatment! We didn't even pay!'

Storm laughed. 'The twins use this club. They never pay, and neither do their special friends.'

Danny shook his head and smiled as he looked around the club. It was just before midnight and the place seemed packed to capacity. It was a long time since he'd ventured into a club of any description, and on those very few occasions they'd been the downmarket sort of place where no one questioned your age.

This one was different; it was definitely the cool place to be. The dance floor was a seething mass of dazzling white teeth and white shirts, as dancers gyrated, sometimes under multicoloured lights, sometimes under black light—UV light that couldn't be seen but turned anything white brilliantly luminous.

Danny had made an effort to look the part after Storm told him that the dress code at the club was 'smart casual', meaning no jeans. Danny was almost always in jeans and T-shirt or sweatshirt and trainers, and he didn't exactly have an extensive wardrobe.

But during the build-up in Hereford he'd been ordered to go and buy a few more items of clothing—his instructors had told him that jeans and sweatshirt wouldn't always be what was required. So he'd gone to the Next store in Hereford and bought a couple of pairs of trousers and some shirts, and even a pair of regular shoes.

The shoes were pinching his feet and he was hoping that Storm wouldn't ask him to dance. His dancing was terrible at the best of times, but in these shoes he'd look like a total idiot.

Fortunately Storm was avoiding the seething mass of bodies on the dance floor and was heading for the bar, where the music level was slightly less eardrum-bursting.

A barman appeared the moment Storm flashed her stunning smile. 'Large vodka tonic, please!' She turned to Danny. 'What about you?'

It was another problem. Danny hadn't realized that a simple evening out could be so complicated. He didn't drink. Not because he had any objection to it; he just didn't like the taste. He'd tried beer a few times and thought it was revolting; he'd never bothered with anything stronger. But he couldn't tell Storm that—he'd feel a right dickhead.

'Come on, Danny,' said Storm. 'We're not the only customers.'

'Er . . . er . . . I'll have a Beck's.'

Storm paid for the drinks, caught Danny's eye and nodded towards the VIP section. It was less crowded and they'd be able to sit down and talk—which, Danny reminded himself, was what he was there for.

He noticed the envious glances he received from other guys as they squeezed through and headed for the blue velvet rope which barred the way to everyone but the so-called VIPs. Storm might not be his girlfriend, but the guys watching them didn't know that. It made him feel good and he smiled as

104

a big bouncer detached the rope and held it back so that they could walk through.

But not all the looks cast in Danny's direction were envious; one was filled with hatred, scorching into him like a laser.

It was Albie. And Albie wasn't having a good night. His Meltdown-addled mind was in turmoil as his eyes flicked from Danny to Storm. The slag! She wouldn't come to a club with him but now she was here with that poncy wimp!

Albie turned away from any watching eyes and opened one clenched hand: two brilliant white Ms glowed under the black light.

*　　*　　*

The red Mini Cooper was travelling at a steady pace away from Manchester city centre.

Fergus had told Phil to follow the angry young man with the flaming red hair when he left the twins, and to get an IR marker on his vehicle—if he had a vehicle.

Well, Carrot-top had a vehicle right enough; it was a deeper shade of red than his hair.

The exchange between Carrot-top and the twins had been pretty short and not too sweet. He'd said what he had to say, listened to what Phil guessed were some reassuring words from the twins, and then got up and left. Phil had followed, hoping that he'd get lucky and his target had a vehicle parked nearby. If he didn't, it might well be all over before it began.

Phil's Vectra was parked close to the hotel. He followed his target up into reception and through the glass double doors at the front. Directly across the street was a parking bay where three taxis stood waiting for fares. If Carrot-top took the first, Phil would have no option but to jump into the one behind and do the old 'follow that car' routine.

That wouldn't be good. The roads were relatively quiet at this time of night, and even if Carrot-top didn't clock that he was being followed, his cab driver probably would. If he mentioned it to his passenger, then Phil's game would almost certainly be up.

But Carrot-top ignored the taxis and turned left, pulling a key fob from his pocket as he strode away. It was a good sign; his car was most likely very close by, unless he just enjoyed walking around with a bunch of keys in his hand.

He was obviously still too angry to even consider the possibility that someone might be following him. Phil smiled as his target took the first left, Gore Street, which was where the nearest parking meters were located. And exactly where Phil's Vectra was parked.

As Phil made the turn, he saw the lights flash on a red Mini as his target pointed the key fob at the vehicle. It was a little further along the street, right outside the pub on the corner. And, even better news, it was facing the same way as Phil's Vectra. That made life a lot easier.

Phil got into his vehicle, started the engine and waited until the Mini pulled away. He made a note of the number plate, which he would later check to find a name and address. Not that the driver was necessarily the owner, but it would be a start towards finding who was behind the wheel. The Mini turned right and Phil pulled out to follow.

Now it was down to two simple factors: Phil's considerable driving skills coupled with an equally considerable slice of good luck.

Phil's luck stayed good as the Mini took a right at traffic lights and then continued across Piccadilly and away from the city centre.

Fortunately Carrot-top was no boy racer. Phil followed him easily, but at a greater distance than usual, until he got held at traffic lights. He waited calmly for the lights to change back in his favour— there was no point in getting worked up about it.

Edging the Vectra just over the speed limit, he soon had the target in sight again. It was three vehicles ahead of him and Phil saw that it was indicating right.

He followed the Mini into a residential area; maybe Carrot-top was almost home.

The Mini entered a quiet side street and turned left past a small block of flats. Phil took a gamble and pulled the Vectra to a standstill before the turn. If his target was about to park up, he would automatically notice any approaching vehicle as he got out.

Phil switched off the engine and waited for five minutes. If he'd cocked up, there was a potentially long and fruitless search ahead of him. He started the Vectra again and made the turn. His luck really was in: the Mini was parked less than a hundred metres down on the right and there was no sign of its driver.

Phil parked a further fifty metres down the street and then waited a few minutes before getting out and taking an aerosol can from his ready bag. Walking back to the Mini, he held the spray can in his left hand, stretched out his arm and quickly sprayed a line of invisible IR paint all the way from the boot, over the roof and down the vehicle's bonnet.

Phil kept walking, remaining third party aware. He continued round the block before arriving back at his car.

As he got in and started the engine, Phil thought of Lee and Danny out clubbing. He smiled to himself. 'Part-timers,' he muttered.

20

One visit to the dance floor was enough for Storm to establish that whatever skills Danny had, they didn't extend to dancing. He was awful—embarrassing. It was lucky that the floor was so crowded and only those unfortunate enough to be very close got a look at his technique.

As one song ended and another began, Storm smiled and indicated that she'd had enough. Danny followed her back towards the VIP area. A second beer was waiting; he was already feeling a bit light-headed but he was enjoying himself.

They found their seats and Danny took a small sip of the Beck's. He still didn't like it much, but the club was hot and he was thirsty. He thought about ordering a soft drink—the last thing he wanted was to get pulled for drink driving.

'So tell me a bit more about you and your granddad,' said Storm, edging closer to Danny so that she could be heard. 'You've certainly impressed the twins.'

Danny grinned. 'Why d'you wanna know?'

'Just interested. Making conversation. You don't have to be secretive with me, you know, Danny.'

Danny grinned again, hoping that he wasn't looking stupid, but he couldn't stop himself. For so long his entire existence had revolved around one secret after another, and here he was now with this beautiful girl he hardly knew smiling into his eyes, telling him he didn't have to be secretive. If he told her just half of what he'd been through, she'd never believe it. All that had happened, from the moment he'd decided to track down his missing grandfather . . . But that wasn't why he was here. His job was to get information.

'Not much to tell, really. What about you? D'you think you'll go on working for the twins or maybe move on?'

Storm's face fell, and for a moment Danny thought he'd screwed up big time. But she was looking over his shoulder.

'Oh, no!'

'What?' Danny turned and looked back. It was Albie. He was standing outside the VIP area, glaring in their direction. He stood perfectly still, just staring at them. A stare that said everything.

Storm quickly grabbed her handbag. 'We're leaving.'

'Why? What can he do? They're not gonna let him in here. And anyway, if he starts any trouble, I can handle it.'

'You don't understand. I know what he's like. He doesn't want to fight you, he wants to kill you.'

Danny laughed, thinking back to his training in Hereford. 'Well, he can try.'

Storm was already standing with her bag over her shoulder. 'We'll go out through the back door.

Come on, this isn't the time to play the hero—let's just get out of here.'

'What about your coat?'

'Leave it. Come on!' She moved quickly away and Danny got up and followed. As they went through the door, he looked back, but there was no longer any sign of Albie in the mass of bodies filling the club.

The door opened onto a narrow alleyway full of rubbish skips and strewn with discarded fast food containers. The rain had stopped but the alley was dotted with puddles.

They turned right towards the lights of the main drag. Storm's heels clipped noisily on the concrete as she hurried down the alley; she was scared, very scared.

Danny was checking behind them as he followed. Suddenly he crashed into Storm, who had stopped without warning.

Albie had gone out through the main doors and was now screaming in fury as he ran down the alley towards them. 'Not good enough for you, eh, slag!' he shouted, coming to a stop in front of them. He pushed his face into Storm's as she tried to back away.

'I want to go home, Albie! Let me past,' she pleaded.

Albie glared into Storm's frightened eyes and made a grab for her, but Danny moved in between them. 'Leave her!'

Albie didn't even acknowledge him. He was in another world—a world where chemicals were attacking his brain; destroying it.

Danny grabbed him around the neck, but Albie spun round and got his own hands around Danny's neck, squeezing with incredible strength as he slammed his victim back against the wall. He started to bang Danny's head against the brickwork.

Storm tried to drag him away. 'Albie! You'll kill him!'

Albie stopped, but only to turn and push Storm to the ground. She tried to crawl away, but Albie kicked her viciously in the side, making her scream in fear and agony.

'Slag!'

The moment of respite gave Danny the opportunity to leap at the drug-crazed Albie. As Storm crawled into a gap between two rubbish skips to find some protection, Danny clung to Albie's back and jammed his fingers into his eyes. Albie yelled in rage and jerked from side to side, trying to throw Danny off. He brought both hands back to grab Danny's head, and with M-driven strength, pulled him over his shoulders and down into a puddle.

'Think you're hard! Think you're hard!'

Danny was struggling to think at all—his whole body had been jarred by the fall and his head was spinning—but he glimpsed the flash of steel and saw that Albie had pulled a knife from the waistband of his trousers. The blade glinted in the darkness as Albie raised his hand and moved forward, ready to strike.

Danny couldn't move—it was too late; he realized that he had underestimated Albie's strength. It was a bad mistake.

Then he heard Albie howl in pain. It was Lee. He had crashed into Albie's back and sent him sprawling on the ground. The young thug was groaning as he lay with his face in a filthy puddle.

Lee grabbed Danny and hauled him to his feet. 'Get her out!' he breathed. 'Now! You've still got a job to do!'

Danny nodded and watched Lee run back up the alley. He couldn't afford to let Storm see him talking to Lee. He shook his head to clear it, glanced at the still groaning Albie and then went across and pulled Storm from her hiding place.

'Come on! Before he gets up! Bin the shoes, let's go!'

They ran, Storm leaving her expensive shoes behind; she didn't care. They came out onto the main street; it was a different world of bright lights and vehicles thundering by. They turned right, towards the front of the club and Danny's car.

Latecomers were still queuing to get in. They watched the muddy pair dodging the traffic as they ran across the road.

But Albie wasn't far behind. Blood was flowing from deep lacerations on his forehead where he had crashed down on the concrete. He reached the front of the club, panting, breathless; his head jerked from side to side and his eyes peered into the darkness.

And then he spotted Danny and Storm. They had nearly reached Danny's Mazda.

'Oi, Watts!' The yell was blood-curdling, seeming to come from some dark place deep within. 'You're gonna die!'

He started across the wide pavement towards the kerb, but Lee moved to intercept him.

He grabbed Albie firmly by the shoulder. 'Hang on, mate. We'll let them go, shall we? While you and me have a quick word.'

Lee had failed to clock the knife in Albie's hand. And he didn't know that the wild-eyed thug was being driven by a superhuman, Meltdown-driven fury. His attacker moved at an incredible speed, swinging round at a pace that even Lee was not quite quick enough to counter. Lee didn't see the blade, but he felt it spear into his guts as Albie's clenched fist punched it home.

'You black bastard!'

All the breath was driven from Lee's body and he doubled up in pain. Albie pulled his hand back and Lee glimpsed the knife and his own blood. As he collapsed to the ground, he felt nothing but anger at himself. How could he have let it happen? He was a professional. He should have— He heard someone scream. Then darkness engulfed him, and there was nothing.

*   *   *

From across the street, Danny and Storm heard the scream as they reached the car.

Danny was trying to peer through the stream of traffic and the huddle of shouting, yelling figures on the far side of the street. 'What's happening?' he shouted.

Storm wasn't interested. 'Come on—please! Just get us out of here.'

'But there's—'

'Leave it! Let's go. Please!'

Danny hesitated, holding the car door open. He couldn't see what was happening but he feared that Lee was in trouble. He wanted to go back to help his mate, but what could he do? If Lee was down, help would come. If Danny went back now, it might well endanger the mission.

Storm was becoming frantic. 'Danny, please! Before the police get here!'

The traffic had slowed; drivers were rubber-necking the scene playing out on the pavement.

Danny got in the car, started the engine and pulled away. And he didn't look back.

*   *   *

On the pavement, two bouncers edged nervously towards Albie as he moved the knife from side to side. His eyes flicked from one dark-suited man to the other, following the path of the blade.

Dimly he heard a woman's voice screaming into a phone. 'Yes, police! And an ambulance! He's not moving! I think he's dead!'

Dead. Albie heard the word and something in his befuddled brain told him he had to get away while there was still a chance.

He lunged forward with the knife and the two bouncers leaped back, briefly off balance. Before they could recover, Albie turned and ran.

'Stop him!' yelled someone, and for a moment the bouncers started to give chase. But then they stopped. Their job was to protect the people in the club; they weren't paid to go chasing through the streets after lunatics with knives. The police could do that.

21

Danny was sitting in darkness at the end of his bed, staring vacantly at the closed curtains. He hadn't slept; he hadn't even tried. He couldn't. He was still dressed in the crumpled, damp clothes he had worn for his night out.

He got up and pulled back the curtains. Daylight flooded in, making his head pound. He flinched and squeezed his eyes shut.

The door opened and Fergus came in. He was talking on his mobile. 'No, don't bring anyone else in; Phil can manage while we're away. He'll have to . . . Yeah, bye.'

He ended the call and looked at Danny. 'It's bad.'

Danny went cold and felt the hairs on the back of his neck stand up. 'He's dead?'

'No. He lost a lot of blood. Whoever made the emergency call sent the ambulance to the wrong club. It doesn't look good right now.'

Danny slumped down on the armchair. '*My* partner, the bloke I'm meant to look out for, got knifed looking out for me. And I just ran away.'

'No, Danny. You did the right thing. Staying would have compromised the whole mission, and Lee knew the risks. These things happen on ops; sometimes they go wrong. When they do, you deal with it and move on.'

But Danny couldn't move on, even though his grandfather's words were meant to console him. Nothing Fergus said would make him feel any better or get over the fact that his mate was close

115

to death. And it was down to him. Lee's words kept coming back to haunt him. He'd said that some day his life might depend on Danny.

Danny had known it was true, but he couldn't have imagined that he would be put to the test that very night.

Fergus sat on his bed facing Danny, knowing from experience that the best way to fight emotion was to blank it out by concentrating on work. 'Lee did good when he got to hospital; gave them his false identity and ACA, and then Phil got a call.'

'Can we see him?'

Fergus stood up and went to the window. 'No. Dudley's people just got him out of the hospital. They'll look after him. And he's out of it now, anyway. Sedated.'

He turned back to Danny. 'Tell me about Storm again. You're sure she didn't give you any clues about the DMP?'

'She was in too much of a state. I couldn't ask any more questions. She just kept telling me not to say anything to the twins about us going out together. They get jealous when anyone else shows an interest.'

Fergus shook his head. 'This girl's got quite a fan club. The twins, Albie, you.'

'I was *working*, Granddad!' said Danny angrily. 'Carrying out orders. *Your* orders!'

Fergus could see the strain on his grandson's face. 'All right,' he said gently. 'I just meant that for someone who apparently knows nothing, she seems to have a pretty big effect on everyone who is in the know. Let's hope Albie hasn't said anything to the twins. I don't want them any more spooked than they already are.'

116

He checked his watch. 'I need to get down to the coach yard; the twins are expecting me there. Have you packed?'

'Not yet.'

'Get a shower and sort yourself out and follow me down. And don't mention any of this to the twins.'

'But what about Albie? I'm gonna—'

'*No!*' Fergus pointed at his grandson and made sure he was staring directly into his eyes so that there was absolutely no doubt about what he had to say. 'You're not gonna do anything. Don't let your anger get in the way, Danny. Stay professional. When the time's right, *I'll* deal with that little shit. Not you. Get it?'

Danny stared back without answering.

'Danny, do you get it?'

Danny looked at the floor, then nodded.

'Good.' Fergus picked up the small suitcase he had already packed for the trip to Barcelona and went to the door. 'I'll see you at the yard.'

Danny stared at the floor for a long time. He thought of Storm. He thought of Lee. But mostly he thought of Albie, thinking and thinking until the anger burned like a fire in his chest.

*　　*　　*

Albie hadn't shown up. He was meant to be on the Barcelona trip but no one had seen him. He hadn't called in and he wasn't answering calls to his mobile.

The twins were in the office with Fergus, and Will looked worried. Teddy did too, although more than anything he seemed relieved that Fergus was on hand to deal with any problems.

Fergus was doing nothing to discourage Teddy's increasing dependence on him. It could only help. Will remained more guarded, but Fergus was subtly encouraging that too: it was causing a growing rift between two brothers who had previously been so solid. Almost like one person.

Now they were most definitely two and the arguments were becoming more frequent.

Teddy glared at his brother. 'It was your job to keep an eye on Albie. He's probably out of his head on M somewhere. You were meant to make sure he didn't steal any more.'

Will glared back; he wasn't backing down as he usually did. 'We don't know that he has stolen anything. Maybe he got drunk last night, or met a girl.'

'Huh!' said Teddy. 'What girl would even look at him?'

'I don't know! I just know that there's no point in speculating. He might turn up soon.'

Teddy looked at Fergus. 'We should have got rid of him long ago.'

'Oh really,' said Will quickly. 'And what should we have done exactly?' He turned to Fergus too. 'Kill him?'

Fergus shrugged casually, as if that was an option he would certainly have considered. But he wasn't going to take sides; they were playing into his hands. As their tempers rose, he remained cool. 'Why *didn't* you get rid of him?' he said to Teddy.

'He wasn't like he is now when we started. He was a thug, yes, but we needed a few thugs. And he was clean; he said he hated drugs. Albie's like a lot of his'—he almost spat out his next word—'*type*:

118

they sneer at their betters for spending their disposable income on recreational drugs, while they go out and waste their money on cigarettes, beer and football.'

Fergus almost laughed. He couldn't decide who were worse, the Albies or the Teddys of this world, both riddled with stereotypical attitudes. It didn't matter; Fergus was focused on the mission. 'So what changed Albie?'

'We found out he'd been stealing tablets for some time. First to sell, but then he started taking them. He got hooked.'

'So back to my first question: why didn't you get rid of him?'

Will provided the answer. 'What could we do? He knows too much. We gave him time off, on full pay, to clean up, and we thought he had. From what we were told last night and the fact that he hasn't shown this morning, we have to assume that we were wrong.'

Teddy sneered. 'No, *you* were wrong!'

The twins glared at each other while Fergus waited.

Will looked at his watch. 'We're meant to be leaving in a couple of hours. Where's Storm with those coffees?'

As if on cue, they heard footsteps on the metal staircase outside the office. There was a sharp knock on the door and then Storm came in without waiting for an answer, carrying a cardboard container with four takeaway coffees of different varieties. She looked a little pale and her eyes were tired and drawn. But she was smartly dressed for the trip to Barcelona in a black designer trouser suit over a white blouse. Fergus knew from

Danny's account of the fight outside the club that Storm must be badly bruised from the kicking Albie had given her, but outwardly, at least, she was giving nothing away.

Storm went over to the twins first. 'Your usual,' she said, taking two large cardboard beakers of cappuccino from the container and placing them on the desk. She turned to Fergus. 'And an Americano for you, wasn't it?'

Fergus nodded and took his coffee. Storm smiled at him slightly nervously before turning away with the last of the coffees and heading towards the smaller desk in one corner of the room.

'We're still in conference, Storm,' said Teddy. 'Would you mind taking your coffee outside? Check the coaches are OK, will you?'

If Storm was thrown by the dismissal, she didn't let it show. She kept up her smile as she spoke. 'Isn't that Albie's job?'

'Albie isn't here. Yet.'

Storm took her coffee from the container and headed for the door, but Will gestured for her to wait. 'Just a minute, Storm. There's something I wanted to ask you.'

She stopped, her face showing not the slightest concern. 'Mmm?'

'The fact is, Albie's gone missing. We've got no idea where he is.'

'Really?' said Storm, raising her perfectly plucked eyebrows. 'Well, that is a worry. He's meant to be coming with us to Barcelona.'

'Yes, it's a worry. When did you see him last?'

Storm thought for a moment, looking as though she was trying to be as helpful as she could. 'It was yesterday. Mmm, yesterday afternoon, here at the yard. He seemed fine then.'

Will nodded. 'Thanks. I just thought it was worth asking.'

'Sorry I can't be more help.'

She glanced at Fergus as she left the room; he gave her the slightest of nods, reassuring her that he was keeping her secret. He took a long gulp of his coffee and listened to her footsteps on the staircase, wrapped in thought, wondering . . .

Then he put the beaker down on the desk and stood up. 'I've got an hour to find Albie and sort things out.'

'Sort things out?' said Will. 'What exactly does that mean?'

'It means I'll do what's necessary,' said Fergus, moving towards the door. 'He's a liability—he threatens the whole of your operation. We can't afford that, can we?'

22

He sat in the car, taking in his surroundings. It was almost like *Coronation Street*—identical rows of red-brick Victorian terraced houses on either side, with the railway line behind the right-hand row.

But none of these houses had brightly painted front doors, shiny doorsteps or new double-glazing. Around half of them were boarded up, covered in graffiti and ready for demolition. A stone panel set high up in one wall dated the terrace precisely to 1897. It looked as though that was the last time the decorators had been round.

He got out of the car, ready to do the walk pass.

The target house was number 13. With any luck, the problem that needed sorting was lying inside in a drug-induced stupor.

Odd numbers were on his right, so he walked on the left side of the street to get a longer and earlier view of the house. He needed extra 'eyes on' time, which also allowed him a fuller perspective on the target.

The walk pass was about a lot more than just locating the front door. He had to take in as much information as possible because he wouldn't be doing it again. He wouldn't even look back once he had passed the house; third party awareness dictated that it wasn't an option.

A group of kids walked towards him; shaved heads and holes in their jeans. They flicked their cigarettes and spat on the pavement, trying to look hard as they kicked out at two abandoned Tesco trolleys.

He kept his eyes down as they passed, shouting at one another and mock fighting. He looked up again, taking in everything. Even if it wasn't registering right now, he knew his brain was logging it all and would help him later.

A car pulled out up ahead as he checked a number on the far side of the road: 27—not long now. He began to count down the houses: 25, 23 ... it had to be done in case there were no more numbers to ID the target.

Inside those houses, behind dirty net curtains, was the third party, curtain twitchers who might very well be looking at him right now, wondering who was the stranger walking down their street.

21 ... 19 ... He counted down three more houses and got his first look at the target house.

He kept moving at the same pace, his head facing forward but his eyes half right and on the target.

There were no signs of life. The curtains at all four windows were drawn back behind net curtains. There was no smoke coming from the chimney and no milk on the doorstep. Not that that meant anything; Albie wasn't exactly the hot-milk-in-front-of-the-fire sort of guy. There was no newspaper sticking out of the letter box and all the windows were closed.

He didn't know if Albie lived alone or with family or mates, but he needed any information that would help him discover whether Albie—or anyone else—was inside the house.

The top left upstairs window had condensation on the pane. It might mean that Albie was asleep in there. The window on the right was clear. That was probably another bedroom. And empty.

Crossing the road between two parked cars opposite number 15, he turned to his left to pass the target door. The windows were covered in grime and the net curtains were much the same. The ones in the upstairs windows sagged.

The paint was peeling from the door, but the good news was that it was secured by a simple Yale pin tumbler lock. Of course, that didn't mean that Albie, or someone else, hadn't thrown a couple of bolts on the other side.

He would discover the answer to that soon enough because he knew now that the front door would be his only possible entry point during daylight hours. There was no way he could check out the back because he would easily be seen if he started jumping about on the railway track.

He continued to the end of the street, then went

123

into a rundown corner shop and bought a two-litre bottle of Coke and a pair of washing-up gloves.

Just across the street was a small park he'd clocked on the way in. It was a good place to do what he needed to do. Sitting on a bench, well away from a couple of homeless guys and some more kids who were smoking either cigarettes or dope, he pulled on the rubber gloves and then poured out the Coke onto the ground.

The blade on his Leatherman was as sharp as a razor. Quickly he cut off the top and bottom of the plastic bottle and then tore off the label so that he was left with a large, clear plastic cylinder. Then he sliced down the cylinder so that the plastic could be flattened into a rectangular shape. Next he put the piece of plastic down on the grass at his feet and cut out the largest circle the rectangle would allow.

The circle automatically wanted to curl in on itself. That was fine—it was easier to put in his pocket rolled up, and besides, if the plastic didn't curl up, it wouldn't open the door for him.

With his hands shoved in his pockets to hide the rubber gloves, he headed back to the target house. And for the benefit of the third party, he didn't dawdle; he made sure he looked purposeful.

Walking straight up to number 13, he pulled the plastic circle from his pocket, opened it up and shoved it into the small gap between the door and the frame. As he pushed the plastic in, he also pushed downwards towards the lock, turning the circle at the same time.

Credit cards might well be flexible friends, but they're not flexible enough to open a door. The plastic needs to negotiate two ninety-degree turns

124

round the door frame before it can push back the bolt.

This method worked because the circle of plastic was pliable enough to negotiate the angles yet strong enough to push against the lock and force it back.

He pushed and turned as the circle bent its way round the door frame and down onto the Yale bolt. Two more pushes and turns and the door sprang open.

Piece of piss. But that was the easy bit.

Wasting no time, he stepped inside and gently closed the door, slowly turning the knob of the Yale lock until it slipped back into place, then stuffed the plastic circle into his pocket. He stood still, just looking and listening, tuning in to his surroundings.

The place was a dump. Dozens of letters, leaflets and flyers lay scattered about the hallway, most of them covered with damp, muddy footprints. Cigarette butts and empty foil takeaway cartons lay where they had been dropped on the threadbare carpet.

His eyes, ears and nose were working overtime. He kept his mouth open to limit the noise of his own swallowing so that he could hear as much as possible inside the house. Downstairs there was nothing but silence. The only sound he could hear was coming from upstairs. A TV was on: the muffled sounds of music and applause and then a woman's voice.

All he could smell was the dampness of the building; there were no giveaway aromas of toast or frying or coffee. He turned back to the door and pushed home the bolt at the top. No one else was coming in while he was there, and if Albie was upstairs and tried to make a run for it, he would be delayed as he panicked and wrestled with the bolt.

Walking down the short stretch of hallway to the stairs, he stayed close to the wall to avoid making the floorboards creak. He took the stairs two at a time, slowly and deliberately, still keeping close to the wall.

The woman's voice was getting louder. It was coming from the room on the right-hand side, the one with the condensation on the windowpane.

He reached the door, gripped the Leatherman tightly in his right hand and grabbed the door handle with his left. He pushed the door open and burst into the room. He had the element of surprise and he was going to use it.

Then he stopped. He saw a body on the bed. It was Albie all right, but he was already dead. He was flat on his back in a pool of blood that had burst from his mouth, his eyes and his ears.

At the end of the bed some smiling TV presenter was presiding over the bloody scene; she was recommending diets for keeping the heart healthy.

He couldn't look at the body any more; he had to lean back against the wall and put his hand to his mouth to stop himself from vomiting. But he was glad Albie was dead; even though his own bid for revenge for what Albie had done to Lee had been snatched away. He shoved the Leatherman back in his pocket and then glanced through the net curtains as something on the far side of the street caught his eye.

Shit!

It was Fergus. He was crossing the road, heading towards the house. He was doing a walk pass.

Danny had disobeyed his grandfather's orders—his desire for revenge had been overwhelming; he *couldn't* let Fergus find him here now.

He didn't wait to say a last goodbye to Albie. He jumped down the stairs three at a time and almost missed the last few steps. He grabbed the banisters and steadied himself. As he reached the front door, he heard his grandfather's footsteps passing just a couple of metres away.

Danny counted to thirty, took a deep breath, then pushed back the bolt and opened the Yale. He stepped out onto the street, pulling the door to, not even stopping to see if it was properly shut. Nor did he check to see if his grandfather was looking back; he knew he wouldn't be. SOPs.

He walked quickly away in the opposite direction, wanting to run but knowing he mustn't. A train rumbled along the track behind the houses.

23

The coaches were ready to go. The passengers were comfortably seated, their luggage stowed, and Teddy and Will were talking to Storm, making last-minute checks.

As soon as Fergus saw Danny pull into the yard, he strode over. Before Danny could open his car door, Fergus had got into the passenger seat.

He didn't say anything; simply reached into the inside pocket of his jacket and pulled out a rolled-up circle of plastic. Slowly he unravelled it, making sure that Danny knew exactly what it was.

Danny watched as Fergus put it down on the

dashboard. He cursed silently—it must have fallen out of his pocket when he'd tripped on the stairs. That was stupid, a basic error.

He was expecting a furious outburst from his grandfather. It didn't come.

Fergus spoke softly. 'I gave you a specific order to go nowhere near Albie.'

Danny nodded slowly. 'Why aren't you . . . ?'

'Angry? Pissed off? Giving you a bollocking for going off SOPs? Well, I've done all that, Danny, and it doesn't seem to work, does it?'

Danny didn't know what to say. Part of him wished his grandfather would start shouting. He was used to that.

But Fergus wasn't going to shout. He'd thought things through. And he knew it was crunch time.

'I am angry, Danny. I thought you were ready for all this, but I was wrong. You're not, and maybe you never will be. You've got guts—you can do it all—but the first rule is, you obey orders, you do as you're told, you stick to . . .' He shrugged; they both knew what he'd been going to say. 'And the second rule is, you don't let your emotions get the better of you. I told you that this morning, and you still went hunting for Albie. What exactly were you planning to do?'

Danny turned away. 'Pay him back for Lee, I guess.'

Fergus looked at Danny for a moment before he spoke. 'You're not coming to Barcelona.'

'What?'

'I can't rely on you to follow orders. This operation is too important.'

The enormity of what Fergus was saying hit Danny like a hammer. He looked out of the

128

window: the drivers were starting up the two coaches and the security guys were climbing aboard. He shook his head.

'No, please. I've been working with the team—I've done everything you've asked of me. I just got it wrong this one time; I won't any more.' He looked at Fergus. What he saw in his grandfather's face was not encouraging.

'Look, you need me. You know you do. We're already down one, without Lee. Phil's got to stay here and go after the DMP. And you haven't got anyone else.' Outside, the coach engines revved and one of the drivers gave the horn a short burst to hurry them up.

'Give me one more chance and I promise you, I'll never let you down again. Never.'

Fergus sighed, then looked into his grandson's eyes searchingly. At last he nodded. 'All right. But if you go off SOPs one more time, that's it. First plane out of there. Got it?'

'Got it,' nodded Danny.

Fergus paused for a moment. 'There's something I want you to take care of when we reach Barcelona—you're going to need this.'

He reached into the holdall he was taking on the trip, got out a small black camera bag and handed it to Danny.

'What is it?' asked Danny.

'A handycam, and there's a miniature PC with a G3 mobile. I'll explain later. Just make sure that you know how the kit works and don't let anyone see you with it.'

Danny stowed the camera bag in the rucksack he'd brought with him.

There was another impatient burst on the horn

from the lead coach driver.

'Let's go. You're in the second coach with Will. Stick with him. Stay sharp and—'

Danny interrupted: 'Keep to SOPs, I know!'

His grandfather wasn't amused. Danny's grin vanished.

'And Danny . . . ?' Fergus continued.

'Yeah?'

Fergus looked down at the rolled-up circle of plastic on the dashboard. 'What about that? What have I told you?'

Danny reached over and picked it up. He opened it out and smiled. 'Always take out everything you take in.'

24

The clients were settling in comfortably for the first short leg of the journey, across country from Manchester to the seaport of Hull.

They were mainly late middle-aged or older men in groups of two or three. A few had brought their wives along; Barcelona is famed for its fabulous architecture, its museums, its sights and its shops as well as for its football.

The trips were designed to be a mini-holiday, lasting up to five days, with the football match as the highlight. Before that there was a leisurely cruise across the North Sea, with a gourmet dinner and few hours in the casino, followed by a drive through the most picturesque countryside, another stopover, and then a luxury five-star hotel at their destination.

There was no rush—at least on the way there. The return trip was usually quicker, with the clients given the option of returning by plane. Those who were in no hurry to get back, or who didn't like flying, stuck with the coach.

A few passengers were still at work, checking e-mails or talking on BlackBerrys, but most were taking the opportunity to unwind and relax. Some drank coffee or Earl Grey tea; a few sat back and sipped Taittinger champagne. The whole package was designed to be as flexible and luxurious as possible.

Fergus was at the back of the lead coach in one of the seats reserved for staff. Sitting across the aisle at the far window from Fergus was Albie's replacement on the trip, George, a lank-haired, paunchy twenty-something.

Like most of the twins' hired muscle, he was a man of few words. In fact, he'd said nothing at all since boarding the coach but had spent most of the time with his head buried in the *Sun*. When that became a little too taxing, he just stared out of the window.

That suited Fergus; he was taking the opportunity to make a study of Storm in action, trying to figure out whether she knew what the twins were really up to.

There was no doubt about it—she was good: she moved around elegantly and charmingly, never in anyone's face but instantly ready with a word here or a brief chat there. Nothing serious—she didn't come over as too intellectually challenging. She refilled cups or glasses without spilling a drop— nothing was too much trouble, and it was always service with a smile.

131

Teddy was not in the same sparkling form. He was still coming to terms with the news of Albie's demise. Fergus had told the twins as soon as he got back to the yard. The twins reacted with a mixture of relief and horror as he described how Albie had met his death.

The traffic was flowing smoothly and the first part of the journey was going without a hitch. When everyone was settled, Teddy came back and sat down next to Fergus.

He saw Fergus watching Storm. 'She's an absolute treasure,' he told him. 'I don't know what we'd do without her.'

Fergus nodded. 'The people on the other coach are missing out.'

Teddy's face still bore signs of the bruises he had received during his unscheduled encounter with the late Siddie Richards and his associates, but he managed a smile from behind his sunglasses. 'Not for long. We always operate this way. Storm switches from one coach to the other each time we make a stop. It gives the customers something to look forward to and stops them from getting bored.'

'So right now Will's handing out the drinks on the other coach?'

'It's not exactly difficult. We're hardly noticed; Storm's the one they're interested in—the guys at least.'

Fergus glanced over at George, who was having another go at the *Sun*. His index finger travelled slowly along underneath the words as he read, stopping occasionally as he struggled over one with three syllables.

'What about Mastermind in the corner there?

What's his role?'

Teddy spoke quietly. 'We always bring three like him. They have nothing to do with the clients, although officially they're here as security. Their real job is to transfer the Meltdown from the coaches to the vehicles of our European contact. That's the only bit of the operation they're party to.'

'And when do you get to find out where the delivery is to be made?'

'Through a phone call after we arrive,' Teddy told him.

Fergus nodded again. It was all extremely slick and efficient, right down to the last detail—including the performance of the lovely Storm, who flashed him one of her sensational smiles as she noticed him looking in her direction. Fergus had a gut feeling that there was more to Storm than met the eye, but he hadn't worked out what just yet.

He looked across at George as he heard the newspaper slip from his lap onto the floor. George had been defeated by the intellectual challenge of the *Sun*. His head rested against the tinted window and his mouth gaped open. He was snoring softly.

Fergus thought about the operation again. He now knew how the drugs were distributed, but he still had no clue to where or how they were made. Nor did he know who the twins' contact was.

He turned back to stare at Teddy. He looked terrible.

'You're still worried, Teddy. That's why you've got me here. It's not just the Manchester gangs frightening you and Will, is it?'

Teddy hesitated for a moment. 'Everything grew

so quickly, perhaps too quickly. And recently . . . the attacks on the yard . . . Siddie Richards . . . Albie. It feels as though it's all slipping out of control.' He sighed. 'I'm just glad you're here with us.'

25

The trip was no longer going quite so smoothly, but it was nothing to do with bad organization or planning; it was simply down to the weather.

The wind was howling, rain was lashing down and the North Sea had turned nasty. The ferry was an impressive modern vessel, designed to stay stable in rough seas. But even the latest technology couldn't control the full force of the pitching and rolling as one mountainous wave after another pounded against the superstructure.

The furious sea had meant the clients' gourmet dinner had gone untouched by many of them, and the visit to the onboard casino was cut short when the spinning roulette wheel only increased everyone's feelings of nausea. Teddy, Will and Storm flitted around doing their best to raise everyone's spirits, but they all knew they were fighting a losing battle.

Fergus stayed close to the twins until most of their clients were either asleep or settled in somewhere for the duration of the voyage. Then, before Will and Teddy could retire to the cabin they were sharing, he took them to a quiet corner of the lounge at the back of the ferry.

'If I'm going to do a proper job for you, I need to

know more about the situation we're going into.'

Will started to shake his head even before Fergus had finished.

Fergus made it clear that he was irritated. 'Don't be a bloody amateur! You're paying me to do a job, so this is how it goes from here. I'm going to tell you what I need to know then you tell me. You decide what to leave out—it's your choice. You can keep your precious secrets. But when your guts are spilling out on the floor'—he looked at Teddy—'and I'm not there to save your skin because you're too fuck-witted to tell me something important, just remember that it was your choice.' He got up and started to leave.

'No, Watts!' said Teddy. He glared at Will. 'We'll tell you what you need to know.'

Will glared back but said nothing. Teddy was still in charge.

Fergus took another quick look around the lounge. It was virtually empty now; no one was close by. He sat down again and lowered his voice.

'OK. Let's do this right. First, this man you deal with—who is he?'

Teddy's face was shuttered for a moment. Then he sighed and leaned forward.

His voice fell even quieter, little more than a whisper now. 'We can't tell you his name. But you don't need that.'

'OK. How well do you know him?'

'Hardly at all. We've only ever met him once. He stays in the background, we just deal with his people.'

'So how did you find him?'

'We didn't—he found us, soon after we started. Less than a year ago. We never discovered exactly how he found us, but he was impressed with our set-up, he had a European market ready and waiting and he was prepared to invest some of his own cash from the outset. He got that back long ago. He helped us with some security matters too—and gave us some tips on staying clear of the law.'

Fergus raised his eyebrows, knowing that he had to tread carefully. 'And you've never worried that you know nothing about him, when somehow he just found you?'

Teddy shrugged. 'We do know that he's a Bosnian Muslim and he fought in the war against the Serbs. He's a self-made millionaire with business interests all over Europe. Not really our sort'—Teddy looked at Will and smiled—'but he knows his stuff.'

Fergus could hear the note of admiration in Teddy's voice. 'And how do you know all this?' he asked.

'He told us, of course, when we met him.'

I bet he did, Fergus thought to himself. The twins' naivety was astounding. Clever enough to conceive an almost fool-proof way of concealing a DMP from the expert security services but dumb enough to fall like ripe plums into the hands of someone who was probably a major player on the international drugs scene. They were way, way out of their league.

'And you think you can trust him?' Fergus asked.

Will appeared to have decided that now that his brother had given away some of their secrets, there was no harm in emphasizing exactly how clever they were. 'We've been making a fortune, for us and for him,' he said confidently. 'He needs us more than we need him. We control the manufacture and supply. Why should we worry?'

Fergus decided not to push the questioning any further, and soon after, the twins went below to sleep. Fergus settled down on stag in a lounge chair close to the gangway leading down to the twins' cabin. He hated boats of any shape or size. To take his mind off the pitching and rolling, he used the time to plan what he and Danny were going to need to cover in Barcelona. He'd got some info out of the twins but it wasn't enough. He was going to have to get closer to the European operation of the twins' mysterious millionaire.

*　　　*　　　*

Danny was looking for Storm. He knew she wouldn't have gone to her cabin while some of the customers were still up and about, so she had to be around somewhere.

If the sea hadn't been so rough, he would have guessed she'd gone out to get some air or even to be sick. But passengers had been warned that it was too dangerous, and there were crew members watching all the external doors to prevent lunatics from taking the risk.

Danny had been hanging around for hours, hoping to have a word with her, but they hadn't been alone together for more than a few minutes as they swapped coaches. He wanted to talk to her again after their high-speed departure from the club, check that she was OK. He didn't even know if she'd been told that Albie was dead.

As Danny wandered around the ferry, he realized that most of the twins' customers had retreated to the safety of their cabins to ride out the storm. Only three men remained in the bar, clinging to their brandy glasses and their chairs as they tried to prove to each other that they were real sailors. But none of them was saying much, and as the minutes passed, they were all turning a more vivid shade of green.

Throughout the ship, passengers unfortunate enough not to have cabins sprawled on seats, many vowing that they'd never travel by boat again.

But not everyone was trying to sleep.

As he rounded a corner by the ferry's shuttered café, Danny spotted Storm by the port window, staring out into the storm-lashed night. She had her back to him, but as he moved eagerly towards her, he realized that she was talking earnestly on her mobile phone. She hadn't seen him and he got close enough to hear her say something fast and emphatic in a foreign language before she turned slightly and caught sight of him approaching. Her eyes widened, but a moment later the sweet smile he was beginning to know so well returned. She quickly finished the call in Spanish and flipped the phone shut.

'Danny,' she said, coming close to him. 'I've been looking for you. I've got most of them sorted out and sleeping. It's just those last three in the bar—then we can sit and chat, if you like.'

'You'll be lucky! I think they've settled in for the night,' Danny said. 'Who were you talking to?'

Storm looked puzzled by the question.

'On the phone,' Danny explained.

Her frown cleared. 'Oh, that?' she said, laughing. 'Just some arrangements with the hotel in Barcelona. One of the clients with a special

138

request he'd forgotten to mention before we set off. Normal stuff.' She smiled. 'Now let's go and see if we can get the Brothers Grimm to go to bed.'

Danny laughed as they walked back to the bar, but inside his thoughts were racing. Danny was no linguist, but he and Fergus had lived long enough in Spain for him to recognize the language when he heard it. Storm had certainly finished the call in Spanish, but before that she'd been talking in a completely different language.

They reached the bar and saw that the three men were still clinging onto their chairs. Storm turned to Danny, sighed and then raised her eyebrows. Danny smiled back at her, thinking that maybe she'd been talking in Swedish to a member of her family. Maybe, but that would mean she'd lied to him and that worried Danny. A lot.

26

Fergus and Danny were sitting on a circular wooden bench that dominated the centre of the reception area in the luxury Hotel Casa Fuster, where the twins and their clients were staying during their visit to Barcelona. They watched Storm glide like a catwalk model across the highly polished, dark marble floor. Only when she had stepped into the lift and the doors had closed did Fergus turn to Danny. 'You have to hand it to her, she looks the part.'

Danny agreed. 'But what part is she playing?' He didn't feel good about the way he somehow mistrusted Storm despite liking her a lot. But there

139

was a job to do and he had to keep his personal feelings out of it. He had to prove to Fergus that he could stay professional and focused.

They watched Teddy push open one of the huge glass doors into the empty hotel bar. He made his way to a table in a corner of the room and sat down to await the expected phone call, waving away the barman when he approached.

Will was still in the reception area. He strolled over to Fergus and Danny and took a seat.

'Our friend doesn't usually keep us waiting for long,' he told them. 'He seems to know exactly when we arrive.'

Almost immediately Fergus saw Teddy put his mobile to his ear and answer a call, making notes on a pad. He spoke for no more than a couple of minutes, then he got up and left the bar.

He looked anxious as he came across to talk to Will. He drew him and Fergus to one side and started on an urgent explanation. Danny pretended to be absorbed in a magazine, but listened carefully.

'He's *here!*' said Teddy, his eyes darting from Will to Fergus and back again. 'In Barcelona. And he wants to meet me and Will tonight.'

'Did he tell you why?' asked Will.

'No,' Teddy replied. 'I don't like it. He sounded just as jovial as usual, but there was something I can't quite put my finger on ... He's never done anything like this before.'

'There's no need to over-react,' said Will reassuringly. 'Maybe he wants to increase production, or extend the network. Have you thought of that?'

Teddy clearly wasn't convinced. He turned to

140

Fergus. 'I want you to be there.'

'Oh, I'll be there. Out of sight, but I'll be there. If you like, I can put a wire on you so I can hear everything he says.'

Will and Teddy exchanged glances. Danny caught the tiny shake of Will's head and Teddy's nod.

'I think you're making too much of this, Teddy,' Will said. 'I really do. Our problems were back home, not here.'

Teddy thought about it, then agreed. 'Just be there, Watts. No wire,' he said.

He was clutching two small pieces of paper from the note pad. He gave one of them to Fergus. 'That's the address of the restaurant. I have to make another call, to our drivers. They need to know where the transfer is taking place.'

Danny knew that Fergus had to be itching to get a closer look at the second piece of paper. But he couldn't. Tracking the Meltdown transfer and seeing what new information it brought would be down to Danny now, while Fergus got to check out the twins' European contact.

27

The Olympic Games of 1992 had transformed the city of Barcelona, especially the waterfront. Whole new sections of beach had been opened up, giving a new lease of life to a district that had been run down and neglected.

Now it was a vibrant and popular area. The beaches were packed by day and by night; on long

141

floodlit stretches of sand, young people gathered to play beach volleyball. Many more would stand and watch before strolling on to one of the expensive restaurants lining the walkways.

The twins' contact had chosen a restaurant set slightly back from the waterfront for the meeting. There was a subtly lit, wide terrace, where tables were set with pristine white tablecloths and gleaming cutlery.

The road was lined with restaurants and bars, and Fergus was sitting on the terrace of the bar immediately next to the restaurant where the twins were dining with their mystery man.

It was a mild evening, so the twins and the target were eating at a table on the restaurant terrace, which was warmed by outdoor heaters.

The moment he set eyes on the twins' contact, Fergus recognized the type. The clothes—black polo neck, black trousers, black leather jacket; Fergus had seen Bosnian thugs many times before.

The man was built like the proverbial brick shithouse—five feet ten and solid, with hands like shovels and legs so thick that his thighs rubbed together as he walked.

He was carrying a bit of weight now—Fergus guessed he was in his late forties—no doubt accustomed to dining on fine food, but he was still in good nick; he didn't wobble. His black hair had just a few flecks of grey but remained thick and wavy and his fingernails were perfectly manicured.

The guy was obviously a big-time player: confidence oozed from every pore. When he arrived at the restaurant, he embraced both Teddy and Will like they were long-lost sons and seemed genuinely concerned at the state of Teddy's face—

he made him take off his sunglasses so that he could inspect the damage.

As they sat down at the table, Fergus was thinking hard. Will and Teddy clearly had no idea what they were dealing with. Fergus had guessed as much from the conversation on the ferry; now he'd seen the contact, he knew they were in deep shit—way, way over their heads. He also knew that there was no way this guy would have come alone. Keeping third party aware, his face and body relaxed, he allowed his eyes to travel round the crowded terrace, looking for the big guy's backup.

*   *   *

Danny was definitely not feeling relaxed. He was crawling through the rocky hills way above the city. Thorns dug into his flesh as he moved towards his target.

He'd done well with the Corsa hire car, particularly as he'd had to quickly adapt to a steering wheel on the other side of the vehicle. But following the coaches out of the city and up into the winding hillside roads had been fairly trouble-free. He didn't know exactly where he was but that didn't matter. Being on target did.

Eventually the coaches had pulled into one of the many huge landscaped parking and picnicking areas which gave a panoramic view over the city. They were designed for tourists and sightseers. But at that time of night, there were no tourists, just international drug dealers.

The main part of Operation Meltdown was seeking out and destroying the DMP and everyone involved, but finding out how the drug was distributed in Europe was also part of the mission. Dudley needed to know who picked up the drugs and where they headed after that. He would pass on that information to his European counterparts so that they could identify and take out the rest of the Meltdown network in their own countries.

As he drove past, Danny watched the coaches pull well away from the road towards the cover of tall trees. He continued for about 400 metres and found a side track where he could hide the Corsa. He grabbed the handycam and headed back cross country towards the car park.

As he got closer to the dead ground that was the target, he dropped to a crawl, stopping every few minutes to listen for any signs of activity ahead of him.

*   *   *

Fergus watched as the big guy ate as though it was his last ever meal. Plate after plate of food was delivered to the table; Fergus guessed that he'd often gone hungry in the old days, during the Bosnian war. There had been so little to eat in that ravaged country. He was certainly making up for it now.

Teddy and Will soon gave up trying to keep up with the big man's appetite and just picked at their food. From what Fergus could see, it looked as though their contact was doing most of the talking, with big, expansive hand-gestures and an occasional deep belly laugh which rang around the terrace, causing a number of diners to glance over at their table.

Finally, as the Bosnian paused to savour

144

something delicious, Fergus saw Teddy get in with a question.

The big man finished his mouthful, chewing slowly.

He swallowed and then smiled broadly before replying.

The twins exchanged a look before Teddy continued, and the conversation proceeded more quietly, with all three heads close together across the table. Then the waiter came up to clear the plates and the Bosnian leaned back in his chair, laughed out loud, reached for the menu and started talking to the waiter again.

Fergus could tell from the twins' body language that they weren't finished with the conversation, but it was also clear that they weren't going to get any more from their contact until he'd finished ordering yet another course. Teddy was looking anxious; Will had a restraining hand on his arm.

Fergus just hoped that the twins would hold it together enough not to look in his direction and give his position away.

*   *   *

Danny could hear engines coming up the hill. He had just a few metres to go before the dead ground came into view and he pushed himself forward more quickly, the sweat on his face now covered with dust.

Four sets of headlights entered the car park and illuminated the coaches. It was difficult for Danny to see if the twins' crew were outside the coaches as the headlights swept through the darkness.

Powering up the handycam and the little PC,

Danny pushed the nightspot button on the camera forward. He avoided using the LCD screen, as the light it generated could give away his position, and looked through the viewfinder. The light from the infra-red torch on the handycam was invisible to the human eye but illuminated the area enough for the darkened coaches and the men to be clearly visible through the nightspot lens. The images fed straight to the PC and via the Bluetooth connection to the G3 mobile.

Danny punched a speed-dial number on the mobile. He pressed record on the handycam and the minidisc gently whirred.

*　　　*　　　*

More than seven hundred miles away, in the darkened Operation Meltdown control room deep inside GCHQ, Dudley watched over the operator's shoulder as the surveillance video images streamed from Danny's G3 phone direct to the main screen in front of him. The frame rate was not good and the images were low res but they came through clearly enough for him to see the action as it happened.

GCHQ is the electronic ears of British Intelligence; it looks a bit like a modern football stadium, ringed with massive satellite dishes. It sits on the edge of Cheltenham. Racegoers get a good view of the place from the ring road on their way to Cheltenham racecourse.

As Dudley watched, the four vans reversed up to the coaches one by one. The drivers turned off the van lights, got out, opened the rear doors and lowered the tailgates, and the transfer began immediately. A human chain was formed from the coaches to the first van. Once that had its quota of Melt, they moved on to the next van.

'It's like an EU summit down there,' said the operator as Danny's images zoomed in on the Spanish, German, Italian and French plates on the four box vans. The registrations were noted and immediately fed through to Dudley's European network so that the vans could be tracked to their final destination. No moves would be made against the shipments until Dudley gave the word.

The operator was focused on the images on the screen. 'He's done well getting that close without being pinged. And the camera-work's as steady as a rock.'

Dudley nodded. 'Well done, young Watts,' he breathed.

*   *   *

No sound of voices drifted up into the hills. The operation was quick and efficient and Danny realized that George and the rest of the twins' crew must have started removing the drugs from their hiding places on the way up to the meet. Ignoring the trickle of sweat running down into his eyes, the thorns pricking through his jacket and the tension in his arms from the strain of holding the handycam steady, Danny silently filmed the whole twenty-minute operation, making sure that he zoomed in as close as he could on the faces of the men so that they could be identified later.

It was only when the engine of the first van fired up that Danny allowed himself to relax a little. He felt as though he'd been holding his breath throughout the whole operation. The vans departed one by one, two in one direction, two the other, and soon after the coaches followed, taking the road back down into Barcelona.

Danny lay still in the dust for a few minutes, listening hard, not wanting to move until he was sure that everyone had left the area. Then he cut the connection to the phone, slipped the minidisc into an inside pocket—just in case the phone hadn't done its job—stuffed the phone and the rest of the kit into his jacket pocket and tracked stealthily back to the Corsa.

He packed the little handycam back into its bag in the boot of the car, then paused for a moment to look up at the stars in the velvety dark of the Spanish night. He felt pretty pleased with himself. After everything that had happened over the past few days, at last something had gone exactly to plan. Danny smiled, knowing his grandfather would be pleased.

*   *   *

As the big Bosnian paused to savour something delicious, he took a call on his mobile. Fergus summoned his waiter and paid the bill. He needed to be ready to move as soon as the twins left the restaurant. Not for the first time, he wished he still had Lee available to follow the Bosnian, but he knew he was more likely to get int from the twins if he stuck with them.

The big guy didn't stop chewing as he nodded in response to whatever was being said for the few seconds the phone was at his ear.

He smiled at the twins as he put away his mobile.

His plate was empty—it seemed he had finally eaten enough. He pulled a wad of euros from a trouser pocket and paid the bill in cash, adding a huge tip for the grateful waiter.

Then he looked over his shoulder, along the road, and lifted an arm. Immediately the headlights on a vehicle parked fifty metres away lit up and the car moved out into the road and cruised up to the restaurant.

Fergus glanced over at the vehicle; it was a huge black Mercedes with tinted windows at the rear. In the front seats sat two heavy-looking characters. The backup.

The big man stood up, delved into the inside pocket of his black leather jacket and pulled out what appeared to be a couple of tickets, which he handed to the twins.

Will and Teddy stood up to shake hands with him before he left, weaving his way steadily through the packed tables towards the car.

From the back window of a VW van parked down the road from the restaurant a camera began to click furiously. It wasn't the first time it had been put to use that evening.

It continued clicking as the Bosnian got into his car and was driven away.

And then Teddy made a mistake. He was a bag of nerves. He slumped down in his chair, turned and looked directly at Fergus.

In the parked van, the camera began clicking again.

28

Phil was driving along a wet and busy road, desperately trying to read the road names through rain-streaked windows. The streetlights were making his task even more difficult. He pressed his gear-stick radio pressel.

'You sure he turned left into Hayward Street?'

The voice coming back in Phil's ear was slow and monotonous; it had all the enthusiasm of a bank clerk counting out someone else's money.

'Correct. Target now halfway along Hayward Street.'

'Roger that.'

Phil kept on checking left as he pushed his way through the traffic, with the vehicle's windscreen wipers battering to and fro.

The Predator operator was having no such problems with the rain. His Portacabin, erected on a vehicle trailer, was full of TV monitors, and bird's-eye views of Manchester were being picked up from two massive portable satellite dishes sitting outside on the runway.

He could see vehicle lights moving slowly along the busy streets. People were just white shapes against darker backgrounds as they walked along the pavements.

But the operator was concentrating on one vehicle in particular: the Mini with the bright white stripe that had been sprayed over it.

Phil had done his follow-up work from the Mini's number plate and had discovered that the red-headed guy he'd called Carrot-top was a young graduate chemist by the name of Freddie Lucas.

Now, Fiery Fred was being tracked by a Predator drone that the operator was guiding remotely. It was circling 40,000 feet above the city.

The Predator, a UAV, looks a bit like a glider, with a wingspan of around fifteen metres. It has been in service since 1995 and was first used during the war in the Balkans as a battlefield surveillance device. It had been used to track Bosnian soldiers like the twins' contact as they fought the Serbs, and later the gangsters when they started to run heroin into Italy.

Unlike a glider, the Predator has a propeller engine and can fly at anything up to 50,000 feet while sending back to the monitors a real-time feed of what is happening on the ground. It means that military commanders can view a battlefield as easily as turning on the TV to watch a traffic report.

And now the operator talking to Phil could easily track a single vehicle in a heavily congested city.

The Predator contained a number of different cameras, ranging from one that could pick out a newspaper being read by someone at a bus stop, to thermal imaging, which showed heat as white. The hotter the target, the whiter it appeared on the screen.

The camera the operator was using to track Fiery Fred was an FLIR coupled with the UAV's powerful infra-red torch. Just like the handycam Danny had used, but millions of times more powerful, the torch shone an infra-red beam down to flood the area around the target and illuminate the invisible IR paint for the FLIR to pick up. The surveillance devices could easily see through cloud, smoke and darkness. For a Predator, it was always a bright, sunny day.

Since 2000 a new dimension had been added to the capability of the Predator. Some boffin had come up with the idea of strapping Hellfire anti-tank missiles and a laser beam alongside the infra-red torch. The idea was that if the operator saw an opportunist target—armoured vehicles, say—he could switch on the laser beam and 'splash' the target before kicking off one of the fourteen missiles beneath the Predator's wings. The Hellfire is a laser-guided missile, so it picks up the laser through the detector in its nose and follows the beam to the target.

This was how many terrorists were being located and killed in places like Afghanistan. The Predator flies so high, it cannot be seen or heard. So when the terrorists leave the protection of their cave hideouts and travel in their pickups to attack British soldiers, the Predator operator, hundreds of miles away, can mark the targets with the laser beam and kick off the Hellfires.

High above Manchester, the Predator was following every move of the Mini, and the operator watched on a green-hazed screen.

'The target is now turning right. That's right onto . . . wait.'

He checked the sat nav monitor, which showed exactly where the target was.

'Right onto Maple Street.'

Phil's voice came back immediately in the operator's earphones.

'Roger that. I'm halfway down Hayward.'

*   *   *

152

In the Mini, Freddie had not the slightest idea that he was being tracked by so many million pounds worth of technology.

Freddie was worried. He was thinking about Albie. The news of his death had shocked him. Not that he would shed any tears over Albie; he was worried about himself.

Like everyone on the team, Freddie had been only too delighted to join the Meltdown set-up when the twins came calling. He'd known Teddy and Will since university, where they had been popular, with their good looks and endless amounts of Mummy's cash to throw about.

Freddie had never been popular. His name, his flaming red hair, his obsessive behaviour, his volatile temper, everything had conspired to make him an easy target for the cruel jokes that everyone thought were just a laugh. He knew that the twins had chosen him because he was a loner. They weren't friends. They despised him just as much as he despised them.

But he was making big money, so why should he care—about the twins or anyone else? None of the team working for the twins gave a toss about the victims of the drug they were producing; about the damage, destruction and death it was causing.

Suddenly everything seemed to be turning sour. The burned-out coaches, the attack on Teddy, and now Albie's death ... Nothing much was known about Albie—it was merely a brief item in the *Manchester Evening News* reporting the discovery of his body. But of course there was going to be an inquest, and Freddie was only too aware of what that would reveal.

He was thinking about getting out while he still could. But that wouldn't be easy. Even though Albie was dead, the twins still had plenty more muscle around for retaining their workers' loyalty. And there was the money. Freddie was good at earning it, but he was even better at spending it.

'One more job,' he said to himself as he eased the Mini down the street. 'One more, maybe two. Then I'll just go—some place where they won't find me. America maybe. Or Australia.'

He flicked the Mini's indicator and began to slow.

*   *   *

In the Portacabin, the operator got back on the net.

'The target is stopping . . . Wait . . . Wait . . . He's parking on the left, three quarters of the way down Maple Street.'

'Roger that. On Maple now.'

The operator watched the pure white shape that was Freddie get out of the paler Mini; paler because it was heated by the engine.

'He's foxtrot, on the pavement . . . Wait . . . Wait . . . He's feeding a parking meter, two cars in front of his Mini.'

Phil drove along Maple Street and saw the parked Mini and then Freddie.

'Phil has Fred. Keep the trigger on the car. I'll take Fred.'

The operator kept the Predator flying in a wide circle above the Mini as he watched Phil's vehicle park up just short of Freddie's car on the opposite side of the road.

'Roger that, Phil. Trigger is on the car.'

He watched the white shape that was Phil get out and start to follow Freddie, who was already walking away.

The operator could hear the propeller of a second Predator start to rev up on the runway in preparation for take-off. There had to be twenty-four-hour coverage of the city: the team hoped to locate the DMP by following Freddie—he was the only lead they had, and the reasoning was that he would go there one day. With luck it would be one day soon.

Until then, each Predator would take turns to spend its maximum of thirty hours in the air over Manchester.

*   *   *

Phil stood in an estate agent's doorway and watched Freddie disappear into an Indian restaurant. 'Loner,' he breathed.

He thought of Freddie inside the restaurant, seated at a table set for one, trying to look as though he was enjoying himself as he avoided the pitying glances from couples and groups at other tables.

It was all depressingly familiar. Phil smiled and pulled up the collar on his jacket. 'He's not the only one,' he said to himself.

It was going to be another long wet night.

The pale, watery sun was rising behind the spires of Barcelona cathedral. It was a magnificent sight, but Dudley was in no mood to appreciate the view.

Events had moved on at a furious pace and in a totally unexpected manner. And Dudley had a long-standing aversion to the unexpected—or anything beyond his control.

The call to GCHQ had come through in the middle of the night. Several terse phone calls later, Dudley was driven at high speed to RAF Northolt in West London and flown out to Barcelona in a private jet.

The fierce arguments, accusations and recriminations had continued the moment he arrived at the safe-house apartment at the top of a block overlooking the Gothic quarter of the city.

As he sipped at a cup of coffee, Dudley felt angry with himself for not anticipating or even considering this development.

And the arrival of the Spanish edition of that day's *Times* newspaper had brought yet another serious blow. The headline made horrifying reading.

THINK-TANK PREDICTS
EUROPEAN MELTDOWN

There had been a leak. Someone on the inside had given *The Times* its 'world exclusive'.

The source of the leak didn't matter at that

moment; what mattered was the catastrophic effect the revelations would have on public confidence and morale.

The think-tank's nightmare scenario—police forces throughout Europe being unable to cope, health services breaking down under the pressure on the system and, worst of all for Dudley, Meltdown falling into the hands of some terrorist organization—was all there in black and white for anyone to read.

And following the revelations of the last few hours, it appeared that the feared terror link might well turn into a reality.

Dudley threw down the paper, imagining the red-hot phone lines between Downing Street and the major European capitals, and the questions that would be asked in the House later that day.

It was a disaster, and there was only one way out. The Meltdown operation had to be successfully concluded within days. Then the government and his own department could put a positive spin on their secrecy, claiming that the information had been withheld in the public interest and that, as a result, an international crisis had been averted.

It would be the perfect solution, but with so many strands needing to be wound up at virtually the same moment, timing would be crucial. They still needed to discover the whereabouts of the DMP, and now a completely new element had been thrown into the melting pot.

The entry buzzer sounded and Dudley heard one of the minders going to open the door.

He sighed; he was not looking forward to the next few minutes. He glanced down at the newspaper again and his eyes slid across to the array of blown-up black and white photographs lying beside it. Photographs of the big Bosnian, the twins—and Fergus Watts.

Dudley had summoned Fergus to an urgent meeting. He didn't give the reasons on the phone; he couldn't. He just told him that there was a 'highly significant development' which needed discussion.

*   *   *

When Fergus came in, his eyes were immediately drawn to the photographs on the table.

Without even greeting Dudley, he shouted, 'You had me photographed!'

He picked up one of the photos and almost shoved it into Dudley's face. 'Someone's been covering me without you even telling me! What the hell are you playing at?'

Dudley shook his head. 'Sit down, Mr Watts. Please? And try to stay calm.'

'Calm?' Fergus threw the photo back onto the table. '*I'm* meant to be running this operation and you—'

Dudley raised both hands. He looked pained.

'Please take a seat,' he said. 'As I told you—there has been an unexpected development which involves a change of plan.'

Fergus sat at the table and started flicking through the piles of photographs, shaking his head in disgust as he saw the twins and the mysterious Bosnian.

'I assure you that I knew nothing of this until a few hours ago,' said Dudley. 'I did not sanction these photographs.'

158

'No?' said Fergus. 'Well, who did?'

A door on the far side of the room opened and a woman dressed in a black designer trouser suit strode in.

'I did,' she said.

Fergus stared, totally lost for words.

It was Marcie Deveraux.

30

Marcie Deveraux looked as cool as ever as she stared down Fergus, almost smiling at the stunned disbelief written all over his face.

Slowly Fergus got to his feet. He looked at Deveraux: she stood there, full of confidence, absolutely assured.

Fergus turned to Dudley. 'You'd better explain yourself. And quickly.'

'There's very little to explain,' said Deveraux before Dudley could speak. 'Your drugs bust seriously threatens my own operation. I want you out once you've given me all the information you have on Enver Kubara.'

'Miss Deveraux!' said Dudley, for once raising his voice. He picked up the newspaper and pointed at the headline. 'If it's a question of priority, my operation will come first.'

'But you said—'

'I know what I said.' He threw down the newspaper. 'But the situation has changed and I am authorized to take charge. I am senior to you and I have the backing not only of my own organization but also of the British government and most of the governments of Europe, including the Spanish.'

Deveraux's eyes flashed with anger. 'That is not acceptable!'

'I think you'll find that it is, Miss Deveraux. It's been agreed at the highest level. You are ordered to co-operate.'

There was total silence for a moment. Dudley took a sip of his cold coffee, glaring at Deveraux. 'Sit down.'

She shrugged, then pulled out a chair and took a seat.

'You too,' said Dudley to Fergus.

Fergus sat down and listened closely as Dudley explained what he had learned in the past few hours about the twins' contact, Enver Kubara.

MI6 had long known that the big Bosnian was much more than a drug dealer. He made many millions of dollars from his illicit business and the largest slice of that money went into sponsoring terrorism.

Many groups throughout the world benefited from his handouts, but the biggest payouts were reserved for the Taliban in Afghanistan as they waged war against the British army.

Kubara had a particular hatred of the British which went all the way back to the Bosnian war. The Brits had been in the war zone supposedly as peacekeepers, under the command of the UN and with restricted rules of engagement. It meant they were not allowed to take sides and were powerless to intervene while the ethnic cleansing of innocent civilians went on.

When Kubara's own village was attacked, the Brits were less than half an hour away. He was sure they knew what was happening—it was happening all over the region all the time—but they did nothing to help.

Kubara wanted revenge on them—all of them. They had failed to give the protection that any human being was entitled to expect. They had failed to prevent his wife's death. And now, with the British army deployed in Afghanistan to assist with the restructuring of the country, he was getting his revenge.

The Brits had been dragged into a new war with the Taliban, who were becoming stronger than ever, financed by the sale of the huge quantities of heroin they produced. And Kubara was their perfect customer. Not only did he buy the stuff, he also gave them much of the money he made from its distribution and resale.

Ever since Marcie Deveraux had returned to the Firm, Enver Kubara had been the focus of all her energy. She had been tracking him across Europe for months. Her mission: to eliminate him.

She had come close on several occasions, but her target was a wily and experienced operator. He had spent years in the field, fighting, honing his survival skills. He knew all the tricks, all the evasive tactics, and he was guarded as closely as a president.

Now Deveraux was closer to her target than ever before. She and her team had reacted like lightning to a tip-off that Kubara was in Barcelona for a meeting.

The photographs snapped outside the restaurant were meant to be final confirmation that they had indeed found their man. Deveraux was already planning the hit; it would be made before Kubara left the city. It might be their only chance.

Then she was given the photographs . . .

Dudley sat back in his chair and looked at Deveraux and then Fergus.

'There is a way through this,' he said. 'It means we will have to work together, combine our resources and our intelligence.'

'No chance,' said Fergus quickly. 'If you seriously think we can—'

'*Mr Watts!*' said Dudley, raising his voice again. 'I have no wish to treat you and Miss Deveraux like a pair of argumentative school children, so please do not interrupt me. You can have your say when I've finished. You can *both* have your say when I've finished.'

Fergus took a deep breath and glanced at Deveraux.

'For obvious reasons, none of us would have wanted this situation,' said Dudley, calmly again now. 'But we can make it work. It gives us a better opportunity than ever to achieve *all* our objectives. But it must be a combined effort, with no one acting purely in their own interests. *All* objectives must be achieved.'

'That's a stupid idea!' said Fergus tersely. 'Even if we were to agree to it, we know her.' He glared at Deveraux. 'She'll agree to work with us and then do exactly as she pleases, and probably get us killed in the process. Whatever she says now, you've got no guarantee she'll keep her word.'

Deveraux smiled slightly and Fergus sensed that she had been thinking something along the same lines.

But the smile was wiped from her face with Dudley's next words: 'Oh, but I have, Mr Watts.'

She could only listen with visibly mounting frustration as he continued.

'This is my last job; it's also my most important job. Meltdown is a global threat, and must be stopped. This mission cannot be allowed to fail. If Miss Deveraux does anything, *anything,* to compromise the success of my operation, then I'll make sure that her career is finished. She won't even get to make the tea at the Firm.' He turned and looked Deveraux directly in the eyes. 'Do you understand that . . . Marcie?'

It was no idle threat. Dudley was famed as the quiet man, unassuming in manner and appearance. But he wielded enormous power throughout the British security services and had huge influence up to the highest levels of government; he'd had the ear of every prime minister for the past thirty years.

Even Deveraux knew there was no point in any further argument. She nodded slowly and deliberately.

Dudley gave a faint smile. 'If my operation succeeds, *your* operation will succeed. So you *will* co-operate fully.'

'Yes, but if I'm to take on your mission too, I need more people. I've got four operatives out here, but I'll need more if we're to tail Kubara and take care of the twins.'

'Miss Deveraux! Let me make myself plain.' Dudley's long years of high command were apparent. 'This is no longer solely your mission. My mission takes precedence and Watts is in command. You will work with him. That is an order. Thanks to Watts we know that Kubara has arranged to meet the twins again at the football match tonight. He's provided tickets for a private box. There are things we need to put into motion straight away and there's no time to bring in backup from the UK—we have to go with what we've got.'

'What—a lame geriatric and an inexperienced boy who can't take orders!?'

'Danny has done well; he's shown he can operate as part of a team—and as for Watts, he's had more experience of missions like this than you're ever likely to see!'

Dudley turned to Fergus. 'What do you think?'

Fergus shrugged his shoulders. 'I've worked with arseholes before.'

'That isn't the attitude I'm expecting, Mr Watts. The operation must come first.'

'OK,' said Fergus. 'But Danny's got a say in this, and he won't take too kindly to her'—he nodded towards Deveraux—'being involved.'

'Then make sure you persuade him, Mr Watts,' said Dudley wearily. 'Nothing must get in the way of the ultimate success of the mission.'

31

Danny was on stag at the hotel, staying close to the twins. They were taking a late breakfast with Storm and some of their clients while Danny sat in reception, casually leafing through a city guide but keeping eyes on the entrance doors and the corridor leading to the restaurant.

The twins had been buzzing with nervous energy following the dinner with their contact the

164

previous evening. Will was clearly excited, but Teddy was very twitchy and had insisted that Fergus or Danny stay near them at all times. When Fergus got the summons from Dudley, he had called Teddy and told him he was going out to buy a ticket for the match from a tout, so that he could be in the stadium as backup if they needed him.

Reception was busy with late checkouts and early arrivals, but nothing out of the ordinary. Danny glanced towards the entrance doors and saw his grandfather coming in.

Fergus went straight over to Danny. 'All right?'

Danny nodded towards the restaurant. 'They're in there. Having brunch, as they call it.'

Fergus led Danny to a quiet corner where they could talk without being overheard. He knew it wasn't a good location for the conversation they were about to have but he didn't have any options. He didn't want Teddy emerging from the restaurant and finding their security had gone missing.

'What did Dudley want?' Danny asked his grandfather as they sat down. 'Is there a problem?'

'You could call it that. It turns out that our operation has come up against someone else's.'

'What—the Spanish Firm?'

'No, ours ... You're not going to like it.' Fergus paused. '*I* don't like it. It's shit.' He looked at Danny. 'The other op is being run by Deveraux. She's here.'

Danny stared at him, his eyes wide with horror. 'What ... ?'

'She's after the twins' contact too—his name's Kubara; no surprise—he's big time—terrorism, the works.'

165

The shock on Danny's face was turning to rage and his voice rose. 'Dudley lied to us again—he promised—'

Fergus gestured to him to keep quiet. 'Dudley didn't know anything about it until last night,' he said softly, holding Danny's furious gaze. 'Deveraux's team was snapping pictures of Kubara and the twins. When Deveraux saw me in the pictures, she put two and two together. That's what brought Dudley over. To sort out the turf war between us and the Firm.'

Danny turned away and swore. Fergus waited, watching Danny breathing deeply, trying to calm himself. When he spoke, his voice was deep with suppressed fury.

'So what now? Where do we go?'

Fergus shook his head. 'We don't. We stay. We see the operation through.'

'So she goes?'

'No. It's now a combined operation. Me in command.'

'What!' hissed Danny loudly. 'You're expecting me to work with the person who killed Elena in cold blood. And you've agreed to go along with this without asking me—'

Fergus could see that people in the lobby were beginning to stare. He had to make Danny get a grip and not compromise the situation.

'No, I haven't. I've told them that I've got to talk to you before agreeing to anything. But I think we should stick with it. Dudley seems to have Deveraux under control—'

'Yeah, right!' sneered Danny.

'We'll have to watch her,' said Fergus quickly. 'But this mission's important, Danny. If Phil can

166

locate the DMP back in England, and we can sort things here, we have a chance of stopping this. And then we can get out. For good. Don't you want to see it through?'

Danny turned away again and stared out at the busy street. 'Not with her. I can't.' He looked at his grandfather with disgust. 'And how can you?'

Fergus sighed. 'It's a job, Danny. If that Meltdown crap gets out . . .' He started again. 'One last op and then we're out. Danny, you know the only way to handle this sort of shit is just to do it. Focus. And leave the feelings out of it.'

Feelings, Danny thought. His grandfather had always been a cool operator, detached, ruthless. That was how he'd survived. He'd seen terrible things, he'd seen friends die but he'd always managed to move on. He'd concentrated on just two things: the ongoing mission and staying alive. Like now.

'Yeah, well, I'm not you.'

There was a tense moment before Fergus replied. He looked towards the restaurant and saw a couple of the twins' clients coming down the corridor. Brunch was obviously over and the twins would be out soon. Time was up.

'No, you're not.' Fergus had had enough. 'OK, Danny, you're out of this. Dudley wanted you in because we're short-handed and there's no time to get backup. He's seen what you can do and he's impressed. But if you can't handle it, you're no good to anyone.' He got up to leave.

'Wait!' said Danny quickly. He took a deep breath. 'I'll do it.'

'What?' said Fergus.

'I'll do it. Not for you, not for Dudley. For

167

Elena.'

Fergus was not impressed. 'For Elena? This isn't another revenge thing, is it? I'm not taking you if that's what you think!'

'No! I'll do it because I think . . . I know . . . it's what Elena would have wanted. She wouldn't have backed out and neither will I.'

Fergus looked hard into Danny's eyes and said nothing for a moment. Then he nodded. 'OK. You're in.' The tension between them eased. 'Just don't get big-headed about the fact that Dudley wanted you.'

Danny nodded and smiled. 'So what next?'

'We're assuming Kubara wants the formula for Meltdown, which means he's planning to take over from the twins. He won't make his move at the football tonight, not in a stadium full of people. It'll probably be after the game.'

Danny thought for a moment. 'What about the twins? Do they suspect any of this?'

Fergus shook his head. 'Will seems to think Kubara's their kind Uncle Enver, but Teddy's worried about the meeting tonight. I'm going to reassure him. We want to make sure they turn up for the match.'

'So what do I do?' asked Danny.

'Keep an eye on Kubara's car outside the stadium,' said Fergus. 'Don't let it out of your sight. I'll be out in the crowd. Dudley's contacts are fixing surveillance in Kubara's box right now; we'll all have a link to a transmitter so we can hear what's going on.'

'Sounds sorted,' said Danny.

'As much as it can be. But remember, Deveraux's gone along with all this, but she wasn't happy.

Whatever happens tonight, she'll still have her own agenda.'

*   *   *

The twins had ordered a cab to take them to the stadium. While they waited for it, Fergus sat with them in the hotel bar, giving them last-minute instructions and doing his best to keep Teddy's spirits up. He asked for the new numbers of their phones and programmed them into his own mobile.

'Keep yours switched on all the time,' he told them. 'If there's any sign of trouble, all you need to do is signal by hitting my number on your speed dial. I'll get you out.'

'I'm not expecting trouble,' said Will confidently. He sneered at his brother. 'I don't know what's got into you, Teddy. Our contact's a businessman. He knows a good deal when he sees it. All he wants to do is make it even better. He said as much last night.'

Teddy didn't look convinced, so Fergus came up with a few more reassuring words. 'You run away and what does that say to your guy? And what will it mean for the business? See him; talk. You brought me along to sort things out if they get ugly. I'm here. It'll be fine.'

Teddy nodded. 'I'm sure you're right. It's just that after Siddie—'

'Siddie was a small-time hood. From what I've seen, I'm guessing this bloke's in a different league. You're making him a lot of money; make him some more. And yourselves.'

Will was up for it. 'You were worried about the

business coming to an end,' he said to his brother. 'You were wrong; I think this is just the beginning. A whole new beginning.'

32

The Nou Camp in Barcelona is the third biggest football stadium on the planet. One hundred thousand people can be seated on the three banks of terracing that climb into the sky.

In the luxury executive box, Kubara was glued to the match. He watched as Ronaldinho gathered in a pass from Deco. He dribbled the ball past one defender, and then another, before chipping in a teasing cross, which the opposition goalkeeper just managed to gather. The crowd groaned as one. 'That Ronaldinho, he is the maestro, eh?' said Kubara, smiling at the twins.

He turned to watch the replay of the action on the television monitor at the back of the box, unaware of the tiny transmitter that was hidden there, picking up every word he said, recording his every movement.

Teddy and Will didn't know one player from another—they barely knew which team was which—but they smiled and nodded and tried to appear interested, glancing nervously at Kubara's bodyguard, big and totally bald, who was standing at the back of the box. He was paying little attention to the football—that wasn't what he was paid for. His eyes were fixed on his boss and his guests.

As the opposition goalkeeper booted the ball

upfield, Kubara got up and went over to revisit the impressive buffet. He filled his plate once again.

The twins sipped at glasses of mineral water and glanced at each other, surreptitiously looking at their watches. They were desperate to know what Kubara had to say to them.

So was Fergus: he was surrounded by Catalans munching on enormous hot meat sandwiches from the takeaway stands. If he had stood up and looked back, he would have been able to see right into the box, but his eyes stayed on the game. He knew exactly what was being said in the box, courtesy of the earpiece he was wearing, which was routed into the surveillance system. It looked just like a Bluetooth mobile phone earpiece so no one would have thought anything of it—least of all the excited Catalans, who were totally engrossed in the match.

Danny was sitting in his hired Corsa outside the stadium, listening to what was going on in his own earpiece and keeping a trigger on Kubara's black Merc. The driver was watching the match on the vehicle's TV.

Marcie Deveraux was sitting in front of a monitor with two of her team, watching and listening in an office close to the stadium.

Everyone was waiting to hear what Kubara was planning.

Fergus was giving a good impression of watching the game intently as Barça put together a neat series of passes. Suddenly, from way outside the box, Ronaldinho fired in a thunderous shot, which sailed past the goalkeeper's hands into the top corner of the net.

Fergus's eardrums were almost shattered as

Kubara screamed his delight. On the monitor Deveraux saw him leap out of his chair as he yelled and punched the air.

Danny heard it too, and got his own view of a victory punch as the Merc driver's arm pumped upwards through the open car window.

Danny sighed. 'Barcelona must have scored. Big deal.'

He was no football fan, and neither was Fergus, who was surrounded by yelling, shouting, screaming Catalans, dancing and jigging in delight. The man on Fergus's right turned and grabbed his shoulders, beaming through tobacco-stained teeth as he hugged him like he was a long-lost brother.

Soon after the crowd had finally settled down, the referee's whistle sounded to bring an end to the first forty-five minutes and the applause rang around the stadium.

In the executive box Kubara was still eating, apparently in no hurry to get down to business. He looked over at the twins, a frown on his face. 'You should eat something—you need to keep your strength up,' he told them.

'We're not really hungry,' said Teddy.

'We ate earlier,' added Will.

The big man laughed. 'I too ate earlier.' He patted his stomach. 'But there is always room for a little more.'

Teddy wanted to get on with it. 'You said you needed to talk to us . . .'

Kubara continued chewing for a moment and then swallowed. 'Talk? I said we'd talk? . . . I don't remember. When did I say this?'

'At the restaurant,' blurted out Teddy. 'You said we'd talk at half time.'

The Bosnian put his head on one side and gazed blankly through the plate-glass window at the front of the box, as though trying to recall the conversation they had shared the previous evening.

'Oh, yes,' he said at last. 'My plans.' He shrugged. 'Well, it can wait. I'm enjoying the football. Don't you think Barcelona are the best team in the world—such skill . . . ? We will wait till after the match.'

In the nearby office, Deveraux glanced at one of her operators. 'Clever bastard,' she breathed, recognizing the tactics. 'He's just twisting the knife.'

It was too much for Teddy. He stood up. 'No! Please—surely you can tell us now! We have a right to know what you're planning.'

'*Teddy!*' said Will, getting to his feet and taking his brother's arm. 'Don't let's rush Mr Kubara. We don't want to spoil his enjoyment of the match.'

Kubara smiled at Teddy and put one huge hand on his shoulder.

'No, you are right, my friend,' he said, pushing Teddy firmly back down onto his chair. 'You *do* have a right to know about my plans, so I shall tell you . . .'

He reached into an inside pocket of his leather jacket and pulled out a thin, solid silver toothpick. Carefully he slipped it into his mouth and freed something jammed between two of his back teeth.

Teddy and Will watched as he licked his lips and winked at them before putting the toothpick back in his pocket.

'The reason for our meeting . . .' he said, his face still friendly and open. 'Well, it is very simple. I am taking over the business.'

Teddy's mouth gaped open. He was speechless.

'No,' said Will firmly. 'I'm afraid you've got it wrong, Mr Kubara. We're not interested in selling out.'

Kubara's mocking laugh was deep with menace. 'You people—even kids like you—you still think you rule the world. You still think we are scared of you. But you are nothing. You are not *selling* to me. I am *taking* the business. You have no strength; you are weak. From now on, you will work for me.'

Teddy's mouth was still gaping, but Will was red-faced with anger. 'How dare you! You can't just order us around, tell us what to do. We're . . . we're British subjects. We won't work for you!'

Kubara took a step closer to Will; he was so close that Will was forced to stagger back down into his chair.

'Oh, but you will . . . Will.' Kubara laughed at his own joke. He nodded slowly. 'You, I have just a little respect for. At least you try to fight. It's useless, but you try.' He looked at Teddy and sneered with distaste. 'Him? He is . . . nothing.'

He turned back to Will. 'You are both coming with me, to my new factory. It is in . . .' He paused and smiled again. 'It is far away. There, you will work for me, preparing the laboratory and eventually producing Meltdown. You will show my people the formula and the manufacturing process. In the meantime, production will continue in England, until we have no further need of England—'

He broke off as his eyes were drawn once again to Teddy, who was surreptitiously reaching for something in his jacket pocket.

174

Kubara smiled. 'Trying to call your security, Teddy?' The smile vanished. 'Give me your phones, both of you. Now.'

Teddy looked at Will in dismay.

'You can't do that!' shouted Will.

'Don't make me have to ask our friend behind you to take them from you by force.'

Slowly, reluctantly, the twins handed over their phones. Kubara tucked them into his jacket pocket and then went back to his food.

When the match restarted, Barcelona again had most of the play, and after a few minutes of sustained pressure, their Portuguese midfielder, Deco, was brought down in the box.

'Penalty!' screamed Kubara—along with every Catalan in the Nou Camp.

The referee agreed. Deco put the ball on the spot and stroked it casually into the net. The stadium erupted: two–nil.

Kubara broke off his celebrations and seemed to be lost in thought for a few moments. Then he gestured to his bodyguard, who pulled out a mobile and speed-dialled a number.

Outside, Danny saw the Merc driver answer the call.

'Stand by! Stand by! That's the Merc driver on a mobile. Wait . . . That's jacket on.'

In the executive box, the bodyguard nodded to Kubara that everything was ready.

He turned to the twins and smiled. 'Don't look so worried, boys,' he said. 'I will look after you.'

Without warning, his smile disappeared and his voice took on a new menace. 'If you refuse, or try to resist in any way, I will kill one of you tonight.' He shrugged. 'It doesn't matter which one. You

175

are both the same to me.'

33

The black limo pulled away from its parking space.

'**Stand by! Stand by! That's the Merc mobile.**'

Fergus could barely hear what was going on amid the noise of the crowd after the penalty. It was deafening. Everyone was standing, yelling and clapping, delighted that their team had scored another goal. He fought his way along the row of seats past the cheering supporters.

As he reached the end, he looked up towards the box and cursed. Kubara was making a move earlier than he'd anticipated. He paused to check that he could be heard over the noise of the crowd.

'**Fergus foxtrot. Danny, you still have?**'

'**Danny has. Stop! Stop! Stop! That's the Merc static outside exit gate. Engine still running . . . He's on his mobile.**'

'**Roger that! If they leave now, there is no way I can get to you! Take them! Danny confirm!**'

'**Roger that!**'

'**Good! Deveraux, we need an air assist to take over from Danny with your team on board. We need to stick with the target at all costs— they could be going anywhere in Europe! Deveraux acknowledge!**'

Deveraux was already on the phone to Dudley. 'Range, anywhere in Europe. And big enough to take my team and'—she almost spat out the last words—'Watts and the boy.'

Fergus was still waiting.

'**Deveraux acknowledge!**'

'**Dudley is arranging transport now.**'

Fergus was still battling his way through the crowd, desperate to reach Danny so that they could take the Mercedes together. They would follow until Deveraux and her team were airborne and could pick them up.

'Roger that. We can't take Kubara yet. Not until we know where the DMP is back in the UK. We must co-ordinate both attacks or one side could warn off the other.'

Deveraux angrily hissed back her reply.

'I *know* that.'

She could see that Kubara was talking to his bodyguard. He was speaking very quietly—too quietly for the microphone in the TV set to pick up what was being said. As the bodyguard made his way back towards the rear of the box, the twins caught a glimpse of the Makarov semi-automatic pistol he was wearing beneath his jacket. They glanced at each other fearfully.

Kubara turned to them and smiled. 'You boys are OK, yes? You look forward to your trip?'

The twins said nothing and Kubara issued another stark warning. 'Remember, I need only one of you. If either of you attempts to run or call for help, I will kill one twin and do whatever else is necessary so that I can leave safely.' He glared at them. 'You understand that I am speaking the truth?'

Without waiting for an answer, he went out of the box and into the corridor, heading for the exit.

As they walked down the carpeted corridor, followed by the bodyguard, they heard another huge roar of delight erupting from the Nou Camp.

Kubara shook his head. 'A tragedy to miss such a match.'

178

Danny had the trigger.

'Stand by! Stand by! That's the twins and Kubara and bodyguard getting into the Merc. Wait . . . wait . . . That's now mobile towards the main. Deveraux, I'm gonna need some help around here. The tracker working?'

Danny's mobile was being tracked by Spanish intelligence and Deveraux's monitor would pinpoint Danny's position to within ten square metres.

'We have you. Just keep with the target.'

'Roger that. That's at the main and turning right, towards the roundabout.'

Danny made the right turn and fell into the traffic, two cars back.

'Target at the roundabout. Pass first option . . . pass second option . . . pass third. He's turning back!'

Fergus had finally made it out of the stadium and was heading towards Deveraux's office.

'That's anti-surveillance! Don't go with him!'

Danny took the third option and the Merc drove all the way around the circle of flowers and back in the direction it had come. But not for long.

'That's the Merc unsighted.'

As soon as the Merc driver was out of sight of the roundabout, he cut across the oncoming traffic and headed back the way he had come. Drivers hit their horns, jammed on their brakes, swore and shook their fists as he swerved his way through the traffic.

'Merc still unsighted. I'm checking.'

Danny spun the Corsa round the roundabout, looking down all the exit roads for the Mercedes.

'Danny has a possible. First option.'

He took the first turn and pushed forward through the traffic, trying to make out the black shape in the distance.

*　　*　　*

Inside the Merc, the atmosphere was calmer, for Kubara at least, as the air con gently blew out cooling air. The bodyguard was in the front passenger seat and Kubara was in the back, sitting between the twins, his arms around them like the kindly uncle Will had imagined. He pulled them close. 'Don't worry about the driving,' he said. 'He's just making sure none of your friends are following.'

The twins looked at each other but said nothing. It seemed that the Bosnian knew everything.

Kubara turned to Teddy. 'Now, I want you to make some phone calls to your people in England. Let me find your phone for you.' He reached into his jacket pocket and brought out a mobile.

Teddy took it wordlessly and looked at Kubara for further instructions.

'Good boy. Call your people. Tell them we need a new consignment of Meltdown prepared. They will begin now, tonight; get your scientists to work together—I know they don't normally work like that—'

Teddy interrupted. He'd been desperately trying to think of anything that might stop Kubara, or even hold up his plan. 'But our security is here in Barcelona, with the coaches. There's no one in the

180

UK to protect the process and—'

'*Enough!* No more excuses. I cannot afford a delay in supplies while you are organizing the new factory. We will let them know about transportation to Europe. Just get them making it. I want full production now.'

Teddy looked at his brother. Every order that Kubara gave them seemed one more step closer to their elimination. It was obvious that he was only going to keep them alive for as long as he needed them.

And Kubara's next words confirmed that every member of the operation was marked down for elimination once he had everything he wanted: 'You will give the names of the two chemists you use, and where they live.'

*   *   *

'Danny has! Danny has! That's the Merc now heading out of the city. Don't know the name of the road but heading west.'

Deveraux look down at the tracking monitor.

'We have you.'

34

Lee was still unconscious in his private hospital bed. His mouth was covered with an oxygen mask, a drip fed into his arm and there was a constant blip from the heart-monitor. There had been complications: the knife had sliced into one of his kidneys and the blood loss during the long wait for emergency treatment had been severe.

Phil stood looking down at him. He didn't know what to say. There were things he wanted to say, but emotions never came easily to him. Not that Lee would have heard a word he said.

So Phil talked about work. 'We'll find the DMP, mate—don't worry. We'll find it and get them all.'

He leaned down and whispered in Lee's ear, 'Albie's dead.' Phil smiled; he knew Lee would be pleased. 'Blew himself up on Melt.'

Phil's mobile started to vibrate in his jacket. He pulled it out and recognized the number; it was Predator operations.

Mr Monotone was back. 'He's on the move, heading north out of the city.'

'OK.'

Phil closed down the mobile and whispered to Lee, 'Gotta go, mate. The doctors say you're stable now. They reckon you'll be running about in a couple of months. See you soon.'

*   *   *

Back in his car Phil hit the radio pressel. He spoke urgently; this was the first time that Freddie had driven out of Greater Manchester.

'That's Phil mobile. Where is he?'

The operator still spoke in the same flat voice, sounding about as exciting as the speaking clock.

'Still heading north on the A56, towards Prestwick and the M60.'

*   *   *

In the Mini, Freddie saw the sign for the M60; it

was ten miles away. He was driving a lot faster than usual. He'd been seriously spooked by the call he'd taken from Teddy. He'd sounded strange. More than strange; scared. And the orders he gave were like no others before.

Freddie didn't like it, working together with the other scientist and in the same place as last time. It was all wrong; they never operated that way. He hadn't even met the other guy. But he couldn't refuse. If he didn't turn up, someone would come looking for him; the threat was always there. He couldn't run. Not this time.

Earlier in the day Freddie had seen the story in the newspaper about Meltdown. Maybe the twins had seen it too, and were panicking almost as much as he was. He didn't care about riots on the streets, or terrorists, or anything else. This had to be the last one; he'd get himself a little bonus by slipping a few packs of Meltdown into his pockets. Then he was out of there, a long way away.

He pushed his foot down on the accelerator, his greed a lot stronger than his common sense, which was telling him to turn the car round and drive in the other direction.

*   *   *

Mr Monotone came back on the net to Phil, who was now clear of the city.

'Target is at the motorway now . . . Wait . . . Wait . . . He's not taking it. That's the target still heading north on the A56 towards Bury.'

Phil hit the pressel.

'Roger that.'

The Predator circled high above the target,

cutting through the night sky.

Forty thousand feet below, Phil followed the A56 as the operator came back with another fix on their target.

'That's through Whitfield, still towards Bury.'

Phil remained calm and professional, but with a growing feeling of optimism. This had to be the break they'd been waiting for. Maybe at last he'd have some good news to report to Fergus before the night was out.

As Phil reached Whitfield, Mr Monotone came back on the net.

'He's turning right . . . right. Off the A56, just halfway from the motorway to Bury. Wait . . .'

Phil slowed down in case he passed the turning Freddie had taken.

'The target has gone into the old airfield on the other side of Hollins village. It's now an industrial estate. He's going into one of the hangars. Wait . . . now unsighted.'

Phil had clocked the sign giving notice of Hollins village.

'Which hangar? Which hangar?'

He was shouting as he turned right off the A56 for Hollins.

Mr Monotone remained calm.

'Do you have NVGs?'

'Of course I've got them!'

'OK, I'll splash the hangar for you. Splashing now!'

Hollins village had come and gone and Phil followed the signs for the industrial estate. The high wire fence was still there, and so were the gates—though they were permanently open these days, one of them hanging off a single hinge at a strange angle. Phil pulled his car off the road just before the gates and turned off the lights.

He got out, went to the boot and pulled his NVGs from the ready bag. Even before he put them on he could see the semicircular outlines of the old hangars as well as the other buildings. He put on the ski-goggle-style NVGs. Instead of clear plastic in the lenses there was black glass. They made Phil look like a giant wasp.

Fitting the goggles over his face, he switched them on and heard the gentle hum of the power pack sparking up. Soon the world turned a hazy green colour and Phil saw a beam of bright white light burning its way down from the night clouds and spreading out over one of the hangars on the far side of the old runway. Like a jet of water hitting concrete, the laser beam broke up and splashed outwards from the top of the hangar.

Phil got back into the car, still with the goggles on.

'Got it. You can turn off the laser.'

Within a couple of seconds, the beam disappeared back up into the clouds. Headlights still off, Phil drove towards the gates. He also hit the cut-out switch beneath the dashboard so that there would be no brake or reversing lights to give him away.

He drove into the airfield, using the NVGs and keeping to his side of the runway, well away from the target hangar—he didn't want to be pinged by anyone on stag outside. He parked up behind a brick building, took off the goggles and picked up his MP5 from under the rubber mat in the passenger's footwell before getting out of the car.

He checked that his Sig was firmly in its holster

and started towards the hangar. Then he stopped. The hangar doors were opening, and Phil heard the sound of a heavy engine. He looked back towards the gates and saw a huge truck approaching.

35

The 4x4 screamed out of the city towards the airport to meet up with their transport.

Fergus glanced at Deveraux, who was sitting in front of him, as his mobile rang again.

It was Phil. When he spoke, his voice was calm but Fergus could plainly hear the contained excitement.

'I think we're on to something. Could be a while, but stand by.'

'Keep me informed,' said Fergus. It was all he needed to say. Phil had only one objective: to locate and destroy the DMP; there was no need to waste time discussing the details.

Deveraux turned round to look at Fergus. 'Well?'

'Looks like we're making progress back in the UK.'

She nodded. As always, she was focused on her own side of the operation, but she was mindful of Dudley's warning that her mission could not, and would not, take priority over his.

Kubara's black Mercedes was now heading north, deeper into the Catalan heartland, and Danny was edging the Corsa closer in the darkness. All the Merc driver would see was headlights in his rear-view mirror.

186

As soon as Teddy had made the calls Kubara had requested, the bodyguard had taken the twins' mobiles, ripped out the sim cards and batteries, and dropped the phones and parts out of the window, one after the other. No one was going to use the phones' signals to get a fix on them.

But Danny was still following.

'No change. Ninety, one hundred Ks an hour, still heading north.'

Fergus had taken over the net as Deveraux spoke on her mobile to her team members at the airport.

'Roger that. Soon as we're airborne, we'll pick you up.'

'Need to be quick about it. That's the Merc turning left off the main into darkness. I can't follow. Get a fix on me! Get a fix!'

Danny slowed the Corsa as he saw the Merc's headlights puncture the inky darkness to his left. He wanted Fergus to know exactly where the turning was. The mobile tracking would fix and confirm that.

'Approaching the turning . . . Stand by . . . Now!'

Danny continued a little way down the road, then pulled onto the verge and switched off the Corsa's engine.

'Danny's foxtrot. I'll use the mobile.'

He grabbed the handycam, got out and ran, as the Merc's lights disappeared into darkness about 1K away.

Thorn bushes snagged at his jeans as he sprinted over the dusty, undulating ground, holding the handycam tightly. His mouth was dry and sweat seeped from every pore; he ran as hard as he could. Getting to the target was all that mattered.

187

He was no more than 200 metres away when he heard the electronic whine. He knew immediately what it was: a helicopter's rotor blades had started to turn and were getting quicker as the engines revved up.

Danny closed in on the target, powered up the handycam, attached it to the phone and started recording, using the powerful lens to make out the details of the scene in front of him.

The Sikorsky S-92 helicopter stood waiting, its huge rotor blades now at full speed. They were cutting an enormous circle through the air and pushing out a tremendous downdraught, throwing dust into the air. Further away were the shapes of derelict farm buildings and a tanker, which had obviously been brought in to refuel the helicopter.

The S-92 was only for the seriously wealthy, the Bill Gateses of the world, or rulers of oil-rich Arab nations—or the top drug dealers like Enver Kubara.

The aircraft had been developed from Sikorsky's S-70, US Army Black Hawk and US Navy Seahawk helicopters. Its twin engines delivered massive power and a flying range of over 600 nautical miles.

There were military and air-sea rescue versions of the S-92, but it was the civilian version that stood waiting for take-off. The aircraft raised helicopter in-flight luxury to a different level. There was room for no fewer than nineteen passengers to be comfortably seated in leather, airliner-style seats and there was a thick, shag pile carpet on the floor—which meant that conversation could be held at normal levels; there was even a fully stocked bar.

Teddy and Will knew and cared nothing about any of that as they were ordered out of the Mercedes and bundled across the open ground, crouching low and running towards the side door.

As he watched from the perimeter, Danny was already on his mobile to Fergus. 'They're going airborne.'

Teddy was first up the steps, followed quickly by Will. They looked around the cabin. It was almost like entering one of their own luxury coaches. But the luxurious surroundings were not what made them gasp with shock as they stepped inside. Someone was sitting at the back of the aircraft.

It was Storm.

Kubara followed Teddy and Will and pushed them down into their seats. Teddy looked at Storm, then back at the Bosnian, and for once in his life he tried to do the decent thing.

'There's no need to take her; she knows nothing. She can't help you. Please, leave her here!'

Kubara simply ignored Teddy's plea. The bodyguard climbed into the heli and pulled the door shut. His boss was already instructing the pilot to proceed with the take-off.

In a thunderous roar of sheer power, the helicopter lifted into the night sky, and far below Danny watched as it flew off towards the sea. Quickly he ran back to his Corsa to make his report.

Inside the Sikorsky, Teddy turned back to look at Storm.

'I'm sorry, Storm,' he told her. 'I'm so, so sorry.'

189

36

The helicopter that Danny was flying in could hardly have been more different from the Sikorsky, but in its own way it was just as impressive.

The Cougar was a no-frills military helicopter. It could carry twenty-nine combat troops, all seated down the centre of the aircraft in red, nylon-webbing seats that could be folded away to make room for cargo or stretchers.

The interior walls were covered with a thin silver padding. It was there to protect the wiring, which lay behind it against the aluminium bodywork.

Conversation at normal levels was impossible; the two turbo engines were directly above the passengers, so they had to shout or talk via the intercom with earphones and mic.

There was a constant smell of aviation fuel being burned and the floor was covered with solid, gritted tar to give some grip in wet conditions.

It was Danny's first time in a helicopter and he was one of just seven passengers. The others were Fergus and Deveraux and her four-man team. The team was already prepared for action: they had to be ready; no one knew where they were going or how long the flight would last.

They were wearing full body armour, with a ceramic plate placed in the pocket over the chest. The plate was capable of taking and dispersing the energy of a round by shattering on impact. Ceramic is extremely tough when acting as a shield but delicate when being handled, so wearers always take great care when handling their plates.

Deveraux and her team had MP5s as their main weapons, with a torch attached below the barrel, zeroed so that the rounds would go wherever the light shone. The MP5s also had a laser-beam box next to the torch. These carried out the same function as the torch but were more precise and could be used in the dark if the team was wearing NVGs.

The five also each had a Sig 9mm semi-automatic pistol strapped to one leg, with spare magazines attached to the other, as their secondary weapon. They were carried on their legs because the body armour made it difficult to draw a weapon from a belt.

The only ones not ready for immediate action were Fergus and Danny, and Fergus wasn't happy about it. He looked back and was glad to see that Danny was dozing. It was an important lesson to learn: you grabbed any opportunity you could to catch up on sleep.

Fergus was sitting directly behind Deveraux. As soon as she had checked her body armour and weapons, he tapped her on the shoulder.

When she turned back to look at him, he nodded down at her ready bag and then shouted to be heard. 'What about Danny and me?'

Deveraux shook her head. 'I shall be operating with my team, as a team. I don't want Batman and Robin getting in my way.'

'This is a joint operation!' yelled Fergus. 'You know Dudley's orders. I'm in command. We must have weapons!'

Deveraux hesitated. She had been hoping to avoid handing over the two Sig pistols Dudley had ordered her to provide for Fergus and Danny. Reluctantly she reached into her ready bag and took out the pistols and just one spare magazine for each short.

'These are for your defence only. For your protection. Do not get in my way! I will not be responsible for your safety if you or the boy get in my line of fire!'

Fergus smiled. The warning was clear enough and he reckoned that Deveraux would be only too pleased if he or Danny got anywhere near her line of fire. But he was going to make absolutely sure that didn't happen.

The pilot's voice came over the intercom. 'He's just entered French airspace. Still staying close to the coast.'

Dudley was overseeing the tracking of the Sikorsky, working in tandem with experts back at GCHQ in Cheltenham.

The helicopter was being tracked through the EU's air traffic control centres. All countries would no doubt have co-operated with GCHQ had there been time to make the arrangements. But there wasn't time and it wasn't necessary anyway. GCHQ boffins could easily infiltrate the systems. They were reporting directly to the Cougar pilot, who was passing everything back to Deveraux and Fergus over their headphones.

It meant they knew exactly where the Sikorsky was heading, but they still had no idea of its ultimate destination.

*   *   *

Kubara was getting stuck into a plate of bread and

cold meats. He wanted to keep his strength up.

Teddy watched him, too scared to ask questions for fear of hearing the answers.

Will had his eyes closed and his head against a window. He wasn't asleep; there was no way he could sleep. He was thinking; he'd been doing a lot of thinking since they got on the aircraft.

He'd glanced back at Storm several times. She seemed perfectly calm and unruffled, even flicking through a magazine as casually as if she were on a pleasure trip; some specially arranged mystery tour.

The helicopter suddenly dropped as it hit an air pocket, and Will opened his eyes and saw Kubara slip a large piece of bread and meat into his mouth. The Sikorsky sank again and he continued to chew contentedly. Will wanted to throw up.

The Bosnian smiled at Will and lifted the plate he was holding, offering him some food. Will barely had the energy to shake his head.

Storm finished her magazine. She tossed it onto the seat next to her, got up and walked over to the sofa where Kubara was sitting. She smiled as she sat next to him, and then, to the twins' amazement, she took a small piece of meat from his plate and popped it into her mouth.

Teddy could keep quiet no longer. 'Storm! What are you doing? Get away from him!'

She smiled. 'Oh, Teddy. I don't know how you could have been so stupid for so long.'

Teddy stared, his tired brain struggling to make sense of the situation.

Storm was still smiling at the total confusion written all over his face. 'You don't get it, do you, Teddy? Even now.'

He didn't. Maybe it was the fear, the terror of flying into the unknown, but he still didn't understand what Storm was trying to say.

But for Will it was all becoming horribly, terribly clear. 'She's right,' he said, shaking his head. 'We've been so *fucking* stupid.'

Kubara laughed at Teddy's bewildered face. 'Did you never wonder how I found you? And how I knew exactly what you were doing? All the time? The trucks . . . the coaches? Yes, you told me the basics, but didn't you ever think that somehow I always knew more than you told me? No, because you were too arrogant, always too arrogant.'

Teddy looked at his brother and then back at Kubara. 'You mean . . . you mean Storm was working for you?'

Kubara laughed again. 'Oh, more than that, Teddy. Much more than that.'

This time both brothers looked at Storm, their minds racing with the implications of what he was saying.

'She's . . . she's your . . . ?' Teddy was desperately struggling to voice what he was thinking. 'She's your . . . your girlfriend?'

Storm shook her head. 'You know, I somehow knew you'd think that when the time came. Someone else for you to be jealous of. But no, Teddy, I'm not his girlfriend.'

'Then what?'

Kubara leaned close to them. 'Don't you English have a saying about blood being thicker than water?'

Teddy gasped. It was impossible.

But Kubara was nodding proudly. 'Yes, Storm is my daughter. The most wonderful daughter any man could have.' He kissed her on the cheek. 'And the image of her beautiful mother.'

37

The Sikorsky was beginning to descend, and in the Cougar the pilot came on the intercom. 'He's going down. Looks to me as if he's going into the heliport at Monaco. What do you want me to do?'

'Wait out!' said Fergus into his mic before Deveraux had the chance to reply.

'Roger that,' came back from the pilot.

Deveraux turned to Fergus, her eyes demanding an explanation.

'We don't know that this is his final destination,' he told her. 'He may just be refuelling. Wait until we know for certain, and in the meantime find somewhere we can refuel if necessary.'

Deveraux nodded. Fergus was right. They needed to be able to refuel quickly if the Sikorsky was preparing for a longer stretch of flying time.

*   *   *

The heliport at Monaco perches on a stretch of land reclaimed from the sea and is a favourite arrival point for visitors to the millionaires' playground of Monte Carlo and for the residents of Nice.

The Sikorsky touched down smoothly and Kubara was quickly out of his seat. His dark eyes rested on Teddy and Will. 'My earlier warnings still stand.' He gestured towards his bodyguard,

195

who had sat in menacing silence throughout the flight. 'If I am not watching you, he will be. At all times.'

They stepped out of the aircraft and Teddy and Will saw the lights of Monte Carlo glittering back at them from the shoreline. The harbour was full of yachts the size of cruise liners, many with helicopters of their own resting on the stern. The twins had visited Monaco for the Grand Prix, but all that—all their past life—seemed a million miles away now. Everything that was normal seemed a million miles away.

Kubara went over to talk with one of the heliport officials and they were left with Storm, under the ever-watchful eyes of the bodyguard.

She was gazing back towards the shoreline.

Teddy went to stand beside her. 'Are you going to explain?' he asked quietly.

Storm shrugged her shoulders. 'Is there any point?'

Teddy was suddenly angry. 'Of course there is! You led us into this trap.'

'You brought this on yourselves; you're hardly a couple of innocent victims.'

'You made fools of us,' said Will, glaring back at her.

Storm laughed. 'It wasn't difficult.'

The insults no longer bothered Teddy, but there was something more he needed to know. 'I still don't understand. How can he be your father?'

The hardness went from Storm's eyes. 'My mother was in Bosnia as a volunteer, working for a relief organization. She met my father and they fell in love and got married. She gave up everything to be with him.'

She gazed out at the dark sea. 'When my mother

196

became pregnant, they thought she would be safer in his home village. And she was, for a while. My father was away fighting when I was born. Then the village was attacked, my mother was killed and . . .' She fell silent for a moment. 'A few people escaped. My aunt smuggled me away and we hid in the hills. I was two years old when my father found me again.'

'But he sent you to school in England,' said Will. 'If he hates the British so much, why did he do that?'

'Because it was safe. Because he wanted me to have a good education. Because he wanted to use the British system, take everything it had to offer. Because one day he knew that the sort of opportunity that you two presented was bound to come along. And he was right. My father is always right.'

Before the twins could say any more, Kubara came striding back towards them. He had caught the tail end of their conversation. 'So now you know the whole story,' he said. 'Good, I'm glad. Come, we are leaving.'

*   *   *

HMS *Cornwall*, a type 22 frigate, was cruising in the north Mediterranean after a goodwill visit to the deep-water port at Villefranche in France.

It was all routine stuff: flying the flag, maintaining the *entente cordiale* between Britain and its nearest neighbour.

But now the crew was standing by to carry out an operation that was not routine: a hot refuel in the dark on a helicopter they were unfamiliar with.

The darkness was no problem; the vessel was

197

fitted with powerful lights for just such a situation. The frigate's own Lynx helicopter had been returned to its hangar, and the landing opal at the rear of the warship was ready to receive its new visitor.

The sea was calm and there was no reason to think that the operation wouldn't proceed smoothly. But when the crew spotted the lights of the Cougar as it descended towards the ship, there was an understandable air of tension around the landing opal. Everyone had a job to do and nobody wanted to be the one person who cocked up.

A hot refuel involves an aircraft being refuelled while the crew and passengers are still on board and the rotors turning. If it works efficiently, it can be completed in a matter of minutes, and the crew of HMS *Cornwall* were intending to make sure it worked efficiently.

Hot refuels are usually carried out when a helicopter is on an operation, ferrying troops to a target. The helicopter may have a range of 200K, but the target could be 400K away. In these situations, larger helis carrying fuel bladders move forward to isolated areas en route and become mobile filling stations.

On a ship, the operation is more complex, with little room for error from either the refuelling team or the helicopter pilot.

Inside the Cougar, Danny was feeling a lot better after grabbing some sleep. He watched in amazement as the heli sank lower and touched down perfectly.

Instantly, crew members appeared on the deck; they were dressed in dark-blue flame-resistant overalls and white face hoods and looked more like members of a Formula One refuelling team than sailors. They ran out and slid blocks behind the Cougar's wheels so that it remained stable. At the same time more seamen were dragging the heavy refuelling pipe across to the heli, along with the thick length of wire that connected the aircraft to the ship so that the helicopter was earthed. Without that, a single spark could lead to a catastrophic explosion.

The moment the helicopter landed, the loadie, who was in the back of the aircraft with the team, pulled back both doors at the rear of the Cougar so that he could check that everything was in place while the refuel was carried out. A cable running into his helmet linked his intercom with the pilot's.

And throughout the operation, a crew member stood in front of the helicopter so that the pilot and co-pilot could see him. His arms were crossed: this signalled that the pilot should keep the aircraft exactly where it was. The operation was not finished.

It all meant that the pilots were getting two independent lots of information on what was happening, visual and verbal, as the loadie made his constant progress reports.

As a final safety measure, the side doors were kept open so that the passengers could make a quick exit in case of fire.

The noise was deafening and the smell of aviation fuel was overpowering. The heat of the two engines made the interior of the Cougar feel like a furnace. Danny watched the refuelling team move around the aircraft like ants as the ship moved up and down in the swell.

He looked at his grandfather and saw that he seemed to be lost in thought. Danny tapped him on the shoulder. 'Amazing!' he shouted, nodding at the men rushing around the heli.

'What?'

'This! The refuel!'

'Oh. Oh yeah ... I was just remembering something. Did I ever tell you about Binsy?'

'Who?'

'Binsy Murray!' Fergus was having to shout.

'*Binsy?*' asked Danny.

'Bins—you know, binoculars. Bloke I was in the Regiment with. We called him Binsy 'cos he wore these thick bottle-top glasses. It was during the Falklands War—we were on a frigate waiting for a heli pick-up!'

Danny shook his head, wondering why his grandfather was telling him a story at a moment like this. And then he realized that Fergus was looking nervous and he understood exactly what was going on. The only time Fergus showed fear of any sort was when he was on a vessel—boat, ship, big or small, he just didn't like them.

'What happened?'

'Well, me and Binsy are walking towards this Scout helicopter when these two Argentine jets come in fast and really low, trying to bomb the Brit ships. They'd already sunk a couple that way.'

'Did they hit you?' Danny was looking interested, and he was, but he was also keeping his grandfather's thoughts off the ship rolling beneath them.

'No, they missed us that time. Anyway, our ship's right in the middle of the fleet—anti-aircraft guns start banging off and everyone dives for cover, including me. But not Binsy. He stands there with his general-purpose machine gun and fires off a complete two-hundred-round belt of ammunition at the jets. Got nowhere near them, but it made him feel better.'

Fergus glanced out towards the deck: the refuel was over and the earthing wire had been disconnected; the refuelling team was moving away.

'So, anyway, four days later, when we get back from our mission on the main island, there's a signal from the navy's fleet chief. He's thanking Binsy for having a go but asking him not to do it again.'

'Why was that?' Danny asked.

'He's missed the planes, but his rounds hit our own ships! The bloke was more of a threat to the fleet than the whole Argentine air force!'

Danny laughed as he looked out through the Cougar's open doors.

The wheel blocks had been removed and as the loadie reported what was happening to the pilot, the guy in front of the helicopter double-checked that everyone was safe before uncrossing his arms and stretching them skywards.

The Cougar's doors were closed and the helicopter took off in a burst of power.

'Great story, Granddad!' shouted Danny.

Fergus nodded and smiled and then settled back in his seat. He would never like ships, even Royal Navy ships.

38

Waiting and watching, being patient, was part of the job, but Phil's patience was being tested to the limit.

He watched a huge truck, just one up, drive slowly into the old hangar. The doors didn't close afterwards. The reason became apparent less than a minute later when a second truck, two up and pulling what appeared to be an identical trailer, appeared and also drove into the hangar.

This time the doors did slide shut. Phil waited; he was far too experienced to go rushing in. It was fortunate that he was. A few minutes later one of the doors slid open a little and two men came out, closing it behind them.

They didn't seem to be on stag; they were far too casual. Phil guessed that maybe they were the truck drivers, come out to stretch their legs. Or maybe they just weren't needed for whatever was going on inside the hangar at that moment and would be called on later. Whoever they were, they were stopping Phil from doing what he had to do.

The hangar was built from solid concrete, designed to take a direct hit from a wartime bomb. There were no windows to look through, just the massive sliding doors at the front and a single metal door at the back.

Phil had made a sortie towards the back and had spotted the door, but before he got much closer a couple of dogs started barking and howling. He saw the police dog vans and swiftly moved back to the cover of his own vehicle, knowing that his only option now was to check out what was going on from the front of the hangar. If only the two goons standing outside would give him a chance.

He couldn't hear what they were saying—they were too far away. All he could see was dim outlines and the occasional flare of a lighter followed by the glow of cigarettes as they chain-smoked.

Phil was considering giving the rear door a second go, taking a chance on slipping past the dogs without setting them off again. Then he saw a chink of light as one of the two front doors slid open a little. The two guys disappeared through the gap and the door was pushed shut again.

The waiting was almost over, but Phil gave it another ten minutes before slowly working his way out behind his car until he was far enough away from the target to cross the open expanse of the runway.

He sprinted over and took cover behind the fence protecting rows of rental vans and lorries. Slowly he edged his way towards the target, avoiding making any noise at all for fear of sparking up the dogs again.

He reached the hangar, knowing that his only option was to peer through the small gap where the massive sliding doors met at ground level. He got down and pushed an eye up against the gap— and saw all that he needed to see.

The Mini was parked near the doors, but what Phil saw at the rear of the hangar was far more interesting. The two trucks were backed against each other with their sides down. They were full of machinery, and in each truck a figure in a white coat was moving up and down, checking and testing. Phil didn't know exactly what he was looking at but it didn't matter. It was all clear enough—Freddie was in one of the trucks, walking around like some absent-minded professor.

The boys were in there making Meltdown.

'Clever,' breathed Phil. 'Very, very clever.'

39

'I want to speak to the Prime Minister. Now.'

Dudley wasn't messing around. He needed to take action and he needed to take it fast, and that meant getting the go-ahead for a second time from the Prime Minister himself.

The PM was actually in New York for a conference on global warming. Now that Dudley knew the location of the DMP, he planned to do a little global warming of his own, in a very specific area north of Manchester.

A voice came back on the telephone. 'Connecting you to the PM now, sir.'

Three seconds later, a much more familiar voice came on the line. 'Yes, Dudley.'

They didn't waste time with 'good evening's or 'how are you's. Swiftly Dudley explained the situation and made his request.

The Prime Minister's official work for the day was over, but he wasn't sitting back taking it easy. And he wasn't alone. There were private secretaries and advisers listening in through a speaker to what Dudley had to say.

Only when Dudley had given all the details and made his request for permission to 'Go' did the PM speak again. 'One moment, please?'

The line went dead. Dudley knew that the PM was discussing the operation. His advisers wouldn't be happy about using special forces on UK soil again. The old airstrip was closer to the third party than the abandoned warehouse in Glasgow. If the news leaked out, the media would have a field day, particularly if the operation went wrong. The PM could even be accused of turning the UK into a military state.

But he knew the risks. 'Dudley?'

'Yes, Prime Minister?'

'You are one hundred per cent certain you have found the DMP?'

Dudley had never lied to a PM, and he wasn't going to start now. That was why he was always trusted. 'Prime Minister, I would not ask you for permission to mount such a high-risk operation if I did not firmly believe the situation warranted it.'

He waited again, and after less than a minute the PM came back on the line. 'As before, this must be a covert operation, with a complete cover story. There will of course be no mention of either the security services or the SAS.'

'We have two alternative cover stories fully prepared, sir. Which one we use will be decided upon following the action.'

There was another moment's hesitation, and then: 'Very well. Good luck.'

Nothing more needed to be said. It was on.

*   *   *

Phil kept a trigger on the hangar from his own vehicle, while he liaised with the team commanders back in Hereford. He gave them the precise location and full details of the target. They needed all the information he could give them: what type of doors did the hangar have? What was the best approach route? Were there any third party about?

Soon after that, the commanders had their own

pictures of what the circling Predator could see, and they watched on monitors and finalized their plan.

It was to be a smash-and-bang job, in and out in fifteen minutes. The heli would land a little way away from the target so that it wasn't heard—either by those in the hangar or by the third party.

The assault team would then tab the 1K to the airfield and wait for the order to hit the target. Everyone inside the hangar had to be killed and everything inside it had to be destroyed. Then it would be back to the waiting heli for the return to 'H', and never a word said about the job.

Phil would inform the team if there were any changes as they closed in on foot.

The flight was going to take little more than an hour, but the actual attack might have to wait longer. Dudley was still insisting on every aspect of the operation being carried out at the same moment, unless circumstances changed.

It would be difficult, but not impossible, and it still depended on exactly where Enver Kubara was taking the twins.

40

The Sikorsky was over Germany, heading north. It was flying lower now, almost hugging the ground.

Less than twenty minutes behind it, the Cougar pilot was doing the same thing, flying tactically low to avoid being picked up by radar.

The pilot's voice came over the intercom. 'As far I can see, from now on it's only farmland or forest all the way to Russia. I think we could be landing very soon—there's nowhere to refuel for miles. If they go further east, they'll run out.'

Fergus looked towards Danny, Deveraux and her team, wanting to be sure that everyone had heard and was fully prepared.

The thrill of a first helicopter flight had long since worn off for Danny. His head was aching from the constant exposure to the aviation fuel fumes, and like everyone else in the Cougar, he just wanted to get on with it.

He was thinking about Storm, back in Barcelona, wondering if he would ever see her again. She would have discovered hours earlier that he and Fergus and the twins had disappeared. Maybe she was worried; maybe she had tried to contact him. But Danny was glad that Storm was still in Spain. He didn't want her anywhere near the firing when it started.

' Fergus and Deveraux were talking directly to Dudley and had been given the news about the DMP and the SAS CT team.

Phil's phone was on conference call. He had instant communication with Dudley, Fergus, Deveraux and the CT team commander. Even Mr Monotone, still controlling the Predator as it circled above Manchester, had been patched into the system. All the main players involved in Dudley's complex plan would know what was happening at the airfield as soon as he spoke.

*　　　*　　　*

Ahead of the Cougar, in the Sikorsky, the interior lights were dimmed and both Teddy and Will had finally slipped into a fretful sleep. Storm was dozing too, while Kubara was using a battery-operated razor to remove the stubble that had sprouted on his face.

He looked up as one of the crew approached him. They exchanged a few words before the crewman returned to the cockpit, then Kubara gestured to his bodyguard.

While the bodyguard went back towards the rear of the aircraft and opened a locker, his boss stood up and made his way over to the twins.

He reached down, laid his huge hands on their shoulders and shook them gently. They woke instantly, and looked up apprehensively at the Bosnian's freshly shaven face.

'We are almost there,' he said, smiling reassuringly. 'Time to get ready.'

The bodyguard came lumbering up the aircraft, carrying several pairs of brand new Wellington boots. Two pairs were green.

Kubara took the green boots and gave them to the bemused twins.

'You will need them. Where we are going is very muddy.' He smiled again and nodded at the boots. 'Green for you. I understand the British upper classes always wear green Wellington boots. And I want you to feel at home.'

41

The Chinook carrying the CT team had touched down in a field just over a kilometre from the airfield. It was close to the motorway, but none of the drivers passing in the darkness had a clue they were so close to a fully equipped SAS assault team.

Suddenly Phil's voice came through on the conference call. 'Stand by! Stand by! We may have a problem.'

Phil could hear the rumble of a heavy diesel engine. It wasn't a good sign. It seemed that at least one of the lorries was preparing to leave. There was no way the CT team could reach the hangar to carry out their attack if the vehicles were already about to roll.

In Barcelona, Dudley listened; over Germany, Fergus and Deveraux listened; in the field, the CT team commander listened; and in his Portacabin, Mr Monotone listened. They were all waiting for Phil's next words.

'That's engine on.'

Mr Monotone came back as calmly as if he were taking an order for a Big Mac.

'Engine on.'

Phil pulled on his NVGs and saw the doors to the hangar slide open. Freddie was pushing one of the doors and another guy was pushing the other. It looked as if work was over for the night and everyone was pulling out.

Phil could see the green shape of one of the trucks. Its sides were up and everything had obviously been packed away.

'They're leaving. We're about to lose them. Need a decision now.'

In Barcelona, Dudley knew he had only one option. 'Hit them!'

From now on, it was all down to Phil and Mr Monotone.

'First truck moving out of hangar, two up—we

can't get them once they leave the estate. Splash it.'

'Roger that. Splashing now.'

Phil saw the laser beam shoot down from the sky and hit the truck as it slowly pulled out of the hangar, crunching through the gears as it gradually gained speed.

It was moving away towards the exit when Phil gave the command.

'Go! Go! Go!'

'Roger that. Go.'

Mr Monotone pressed a button on his console, and instantly a Hellfire rocket motor ignited and the missile pulled away from the Predator's wings. The detector in its nose swished about, trying to locate the laser beam it was to follow. It didn't take long: after a couple of seconds the Hellfire tilted downward and rocketed towards the earth.

Dudley had known there was no longer any chance of a co-ordinated attack. He had to deploy the Hellfires. The SAS CT team might as well pack up and go home. All Dudley could hope for now was that the attack would be swift and final.

Phil waited. The Predator was far too high in the sky for anyone on the ground to know that the deadly missile was on its way. The laser beam followed the truck as it moved along the airstrip road, splashing over the sides as it broke up on the roof.

'That's the second truck now pulling out of the hangar.'

The missile made contact with the first truck about five seconds after locking on to the laser.

There was a brilliant flash of light and an ear-splitting thud. The shock wave of the detonation made Phil drop to the ground as he saw the trailer end of the truck lift into the air. It dropped back to the ground and the whole vehicle exploded into a fireball.

'Take the second!' yelled Phil into his phone. 'The second truck!'

Mr Monotone didn't go in for long conversations.

'Roger that.'

Phil looked up to see the laser beam move across to the second truck. The driver had screeched to a standstill just outside the hangar when he saw the first vehicle explode. He was still in the vehicle, obviously panicking, not knowing whether to put his foot down or sit still or get out and run.

He didn't get a chance to make up his mind. Within seconds the second truck erupted into a fireball and the shock waves knocked Phil back down onto the ground.

He could feel the heat of the burning trucks against his body and when he looked up, he saw the flames from the second truck licking back into the hangar itself. He had no further need of his NVGs—the whole area was lit up by the flames.

But there was no sign of Fiery Fred. Maybe he was cowering somewhere inside the hangar.

Phil picked up his MP5 to finish the job when suddenly the Mini burst from the hangar like a Formula One Ferrari. In the light of the flames, Phil could see that Freddie was driving, clinging onto the steering wheel with one hand and frantically dialling his mobile with the other. The number he dialled didn't even ring. The phone was lying in pieces on a Spanish road.

Mr Monotone came back.

211

'The Mini is getting away. You want that stopped?'

'Do it!'

The Mini was already being splashed. It was just passing the first truck when the missile hit and the vehicle jumped into the air, turning into a fireball as it landed on its roof.

Mr Monotone was as cool as ever when he came back.

'All targets destroyed. What's that noise?'

Phil smiled. 'Dogs. They're going ape-shit.'

42

The mud was thick and black, exactly as Kubara had warned. It sucked at their Wellington boots as they followed his torch beam through the woods. Finally, through the pitch darkness ahead, they saw a light, and as they approached it, they realized that it was shining outside a long, single-storey building at the centre of a clearing.

Teddy and Will hesitated as Kubara and Storm entered the clearing, but the huge bodyguard pushed them roughly forward.

A welcoming committee of four more of Kubara's heavies, all holding Russian AK47 assault rifles, stood waiting outside the building. It didn't look like an industrial building; it was more likely a farm building of some sort.

Kubara glanced back and saw that the twins were shivering, and it wasn't just because of the biting wind that cut through the trees like a knife.

'Don't worry,' he called back to them. 'It's much

warmer inside.'

The guards stood aside as Kubara pushed open the door and led the way inside.

It was warmer, and brightly lit. Teddy and Will pulled off the boots, replaced them with their own shoes and looked around. They were in a lobby area; a corridor ran along the front of the building. Another, directly ahead, evidently led to more rooms at the rear.

The constant throb of a generator, which must have been supplying the light and the warmth, was suddenly drowned out by the noise of the Sikorsky taking off.

Teddy had lapsed into a listless silence again, but Will was still asking questions. 'Where are we? And what is this place?'

'We are in Germany, just. And this place? Once it was for chickens—many thousands of chickens.' Kubara sniffed the air. 'We try and try, but we can never quite lose the smell of their shit. Now, it is all for you.'

'You mean we have to live here?'

Kubara shrugged. 'Live here and work here. For a little while. There is a house nearby, through the forest, and later perhaps we move you there. If you work hard, as I know you will. But for now you will find this is perfectly comfortable; it has everything you need.'

Will glanced at his brother and then turned to look at Storm. Her blue eyes were cold and her voice was hard when she spoke. 'I won't be staying to keep you company,' she told him. 'I shall be going home tomorr—' She checked her watch. 'A little later today.'

'And where is home?'

Storm smiled. 'A long way away.'

'My daughter deserves a long holiday,' said Kubara proudly. 'But you must work. In a few hours your new colleagues will arrive, and you will teach them everything. I will show you around and then I think you should rest for a little while.'

Will glanced towards the door, wondering if even now it would be better to risk trying to make a run for it.

'Don't even think of it, Will,' Kubara warned him. 'There is nowhere to run to and no one is coming to help you. Not even your friend, Mr Watts.'

The twins looked at each other hopelessly. They had realized long ago that there was no hope of rescue from Fergus.

'Of course I knew about him,' said Kubara. 'I was going to kill him, but Storm likes the boy, Danny.' He smiled at his daughter. 'And I can never refuse anything she asks me. Now, you must see your new laboratory. I know you will like it.'

*   *   *

The Cougar pilot had found a landing place—it was a clearing in a dip in the ground, close to a small river that wound through the forest.

The target building was around eight hundred metres away. The lower ground and the tall trees would have shielded the noise of the Cougar landing, but the pilot knew it was as close as he could risk going.

He was giving the team the longitude and latitude of the target, which they were entering in their handheld sat navs. This meant that they could pinpoint the exact location of the target.

Once the team moved, the sat navs would guide them, giving constant updates on their location as they went. Civilian sat navs only show the position of something to within ten metres; military versions fix it to one metre.

The Cougar's engines were still running and would remain running, the rotors turning, until the team had completed its mission and was ready to lift off again. Helis rarely close down in the field: failure to restart the engines could put an operation in danger.

Deveraux's team was ready to move. It had its own commander, who would be giving the orders once the team reached the FAP; even Fergus and Deveraux would follow those orders. The team knew precisely what was required, but it was up to the team commander to make the decisions on *how* it was carried out.

But before the doors slid back, Deveraux had a few last words of warning for Fergus and Danny. 'Do *not*, in any way, interfere with the way the attack is carried out,' she told them. 'You will stay behind the team and myself at all times. If you get in the way, you'll jeopardize the objective of taking out Kubara and put your own lives at risk.'

Danny smiled. 'Yeah, you'd like that, wouldn't you. Suit you perfectly.'

Fergus looked at his grandson and shook his head. He knew that Deveraux, technically at least, had every right to say what she was saying. He'd been in these team situations himself many times before. The team works like a machine, with each part depending on the other parts to function efficiently.

But that didn't mean that Fergus was prepared to allow his own side of the operation to be put at risk. He had a job to finish too. He was there to make sure the twins were killed.

He nodded at Deveraux. Then the heli's doors slid back and the attack was on.

43

As Danny hit the ground and started to run, he felt his legs buckle and almost give way. The long hours of sitting in the heli doing nothing had taken their toll, but he forced himself on, and the strength in his legs soon began to return.

The team commander had decided that there would be no tactical approach to the target: they would simply run as fast as they could—the attack had to start as quickly as possible if they were to reach Kubara before he found out about the destruction of the DMP. He might well not remain where he was; he might even have a car here. The team had to act fast.

Each member had their personal communications. They would pick up any orders from their commander in their earpiece once they reached the FAP and got a sighting of exactly what lay ahead of them.

Danny moved as swiftly as anyone, running upwards through the woods. He had always been a good runner, so keeping pace with the others was not a problem.

Fergus wasn't finding it so easy. He kept himself very fit, but not only was he a lot older than everyone else; he'd taken two bullets in his right thigh. He simply couldn't run any more.

The FAP was a shallow drainage ditch on the edge of the wooded area. Directly ahead was open ground and about 200 metres away stood a low building.

By the time Fergus reached the FAP, the team was already lying in the ditch, looking at the long dark shape of the target through their NVGs. They could hear a generator humming and saw lights shining from a couple of windows at the front of the building. There was no sign of movement outside.

It was bitterly cold, and the icy wind cutting across the clearing was making the surrounding tall trees sway and rustle. The noise was good; anything that muffled the sound of the approaching team could only help.

Danny saw that Deveraux was talking to the team commander; they were searching for all possible entry points. The principle of all room combat is to get as many of the team as possible into the target at one time. That way, the team quickly swamps the inside of the building so that the x-rays within do not have time to react.

The team commander had clocked the two doors at either end of the building. They were closed but he had no idea whether or not they were locked.

That wouldn't be a problem: each team member had an explosive door-entry charge in the back pouch of their body armour.

As the team prepared the charges, Deveraux looked back and frowned at Fergus as he finally reached the ditch; then she whispered a few words to the commander, who nodded and turned to the big man on his other side.

Deveraux got up and went over to Fergus. 'You're out of this, Watts,' she told him. 'You're even more of a liability than I remembered—you can hardly move. You're going to put the rest of us at risk if you can't keep up.'

'No! I'm here to do a job, just like you.'

Danny had been lying in the ditch with the others, but now he rose to a crouch and went over to join his grandfather and Deveraux. 'What's going on?' he asked.

'I want you to take Grandpa here back to the heli. He's a liability, and so are you. I should never have agreed to you even getting on board.'

'We're part of this mission, Deveraux,' Fergus insisted. 'You know Dudley's orders.'

'Dudley isn't here. I'll give Dudley what he wants, but I'll do it *my* way.'

'Look, Deveraux—'

As they focused on Deveraux, neither Fergus nor Danny had spotted the big guy coming up behind them. He'd pulled a telescopic steel truncheon out from under his body armour. As he approached, Deveraux nodded to him, and in one swift movement he raised the baton and brought it crashing down into Fergus's right kneecap.

Fergus went down, and his sharp cry of pain was carried away on the wind.

Danny instinctively moved to reach for his Sig, but the big guy grabbed his arm.

'You know that isn't wise, Danny,' said Deveraux. 'You know you can't compromise the mission.'

Danny knew she was right; the mission had to go ahead, whatever Deveraux did. Dudley would sort her out later. He moved his hand away from the

218

pistol and bent down to talk to Fergus, who was clutching his knee. The patella was clearly broken and Fergus would barely be able to make it back to the helicopter.

The big guy put away the baton and looked down at Fergus. 'Sorry, mate. Orders.'

Deveraux was a lot less sympathetic as she watched Fergus grimace with pain. 'You're lucky I didn't have you shot, Watts.' She glared at Danny. 'Get him back to the heli, and stay there until this is over.' She was shaking her head dismissively as she turned away. 'An old man and a boy soldier. Pathetic.'

The commander and the rest of the team had stayed out of the exchange; they were only concerned with their mission. As Deveraux rejoined him, the commander was issuing his orders.

'Rolling start line,' he told them.

It meant they would all be going for the target as quickly as they could: they would split into two teams, each targeting one of the doors. The aim was to reach the doors, place the charges if necessary, and make an entry before anyone knew they were there.

But a rolling start line also meant that they would be vulnerable to attack as they crossed the open ground. The objective would be the same— to get through those doors as quickly as possible— but if they were spotted, they would have to fight their way to the doors across open ground. They were the only known points of entry.

The team commander checked that everyone was ready.

'Go!'

44

The two assault groups moved off. Deveraux followed about five metres behind the team aiming for the left-hand door.

Danny watched them go and then looked down at his grandfather. 'Can you get back to the heli on your own?' he asked.

Pain was nothing new to Fergus. His right leg had taken so much damage over the years, it deserved a chapter all of its own in a medical textbook. He was in agony, but his mind was still perfectly clear. 'You're not going anywhere without me,' he breathed through gritted teeth.

'I've got to, Granddad. I've got to see this through, like you said. I'm not letting Deveraux take this away from me too.'

But Fergus was afraid that without him there to watch over his grandson, Danny might well become just another target for Deveraux. 'Stay with me, Danny. Please.'

But Danny wasn't listening. 'Can you make it back?' he demanded.

Fergus nodded, realizing that it was useless trying to stop Danny. 'Even if it means crawling all the way.'

The two assault groups were about halfway across the clearing when rapid flashes from AK47 muzzles erupted from the windows and the sound of automatic fire filled the air.

Danny was already in open ground, going left, following Deveraux.

She had taken cover as the automatic fire started

and was crawling through the mud towards the rest of the team, who were returning fire. As Danny approached, he saw one of the team take a round and go down.

The man's partner was the team commander. He could do nothing for his mate at that moment: he still had to take the fight to the enemy and reach the door. The team was firing and moving, firing and moving, just like Danny and Lee had done at the vehicle range. There was always someone getting rounds down at the muzzle flashes in front of them while the others moved forward.

Danny kept running towards the fire almost as if it wasn't there. His feet sank into the mud with each step as rounds thudded down and buried themselves in the ground all around him.

He was scared, but he knew there was nothing he could do about it so he just kept going.

His eyes were fixed on Deveraux, who was crouched down in front of him. As she looked back at the man down, she spotted Danny coming up behind her. She swore, then got up and started off towards the target again. Danny saw that she had lost her MP5. He guessed that it must have been swallowed up in the mud as she threw herself to the ground.

Danny reached the man down and saw that it was the guy who'd felled Fergus with the baton. His left leg was wet with blood and his face was screwed up in pain as he jammed a field dressing into the wound. Danny knew full well that the best way to help him was to leave him there. That was why the team commander had simply gone on towards the target: the quicker the fire fight was over, the sooner the man down would get proper medical

221

attention.

'Go,' he hissed at Danny through gritted teeth. 'Get on with it.'

Danny nodded and ran on, head down, the mud clutching at his feet with each step. The remaining team members were still taking the fight forward, but Danny had lost sight of Deveraux. He dropped down into the icy mud and his eyes scanned the area. Then he spotted her crawling out to the left of the target. And wherever Deveraux went, Danny was going too.

As Danny made his way out wide, he turned to glimpse the fire fight raging between the team and whoever was in the building. The team were finally making ground.

Danny crawled along on his belly until he was almost a hundred metres away from the contact. He was alone in the darkness. He could no longer see Deveraux, but she was obviously seeking out another way in at the back of the building. The team had to carry out their orders: the objective was to enter through those doors at the front. But Deveraux was looking for other options.

Danny got up, his jeans heavily caked in wet mud, and ran round to the rear of the building. It was almost in darkness; no light shone through any of the windows, but a small glimmer was coming from a single door towards the far end. It was ajar, and as Danny approached, he could see that it opened inwards.

He pressed himself against the wall on the hinge side of the door. Drawing down his Sig, he sucked in oxygen, trying to stop his chest from heaving so that he would be able to make his shots accurate.

He curled the three lower fingers of his right

hand around the pistol grip. His index finger rested lightly on the trigger, inside the trigger guard.

His mind was working swiftly, running through the vital details he had learned in training and from his grandfather. Briefly he thought of Fergus; he hoped he'd manage to make his way back to the heli safely.

Danny could hear the fire fight continuing on the far side of the building. He couldn't worry about that now. He brought the Sig up into the aim and pushed open the door.

45

Kubara had considered making a run for it when the firing started, but everything had happened too quickly. One of his heavies had come to tell him to stay put while they dealt with the attack.

The large room that Kubara had earmarked for the laboratory was at the back of the building; it had no windows, just artificial light—he had wanted the twins to concentrate on their work. But it meant that he couldn't see what was going on outside.

He listened to the fire fight and cursed. In any other circumstances he would have been alongside his men, at the forefront of the battle. But this time he had Storm to consider. She was infinitely precious to Kubara and he would willingly have given his own life for her.

The situation was bad, but not desperate. Not yet. The enemy, whoever they were, had not yet entered the building, and his own men were good, hand picked. They might well finish off the attackers before they even made it inside.

Briefly Kubara wondered who they were and how they had picked up his trail. He shook his head— he didn't have time to speculate now. He decided that if they did get inside, this room at the rear of the building would be his final battleground.

His personal bodyguard was still with him, armed now with an AK47. Storm was standing close to her father. She smiled at him confidently, and he smiled back and nodded, attempting to reassure her that everything would be all right.

The twins were sitting down, huddled together in the furthest corner of the room, as far away from the door as possible.

Kubara glared at them, brandishing his own pistol in their direction. 'Get up!'

Teddy and Will scrambled to their feet, terrified for a moment that the Bosnian was about to put bullets into their heads.

'Move over there! Quickly!'

He motioned with the pistol, showing the twins exactly where he wanted them to go.

Slowly they moved closer to the door, realizing that Kubara was using them as his first line of defence. If anyone burst into the room, the twins would surely be their first target.

Kubara made sure that he and Storm were behind the door if it opened, giving him time to react to anyone appearing in the doorway.

The twins stood side by side, shaking with fear. Teddy reached for his brother's hand and gripped it. Tightly.

*　　　*　　　*

224

Danny moved from the doorway into a narrow, dimly lit hallway leading to a corridor. His left hand joined the other on the Sig. Eyes and mouth open, he looked and listened.

He edged carefully into the corridor. To his left was a door that must give access to the front of the building: the sounds of automatic fire clearly came from that direction. To his right, the corridor stretched away with a number of rooms on each side, their doors open.

As he moved slowly down the long corridor, he saw movement to his right, in one of the rooms. He turned, finger on the trigger, taking first pressure, ready to fire at the centre of the mass that was moving towards him.

It was Deveraux; her own weapon was raised in exactly the same way as Danny's.

Their eyes locked onto each other, and then Deveraux's head flicked to one side, telling Danny wordlessly to continue checking the other rooms. It appeared that finally, after all their conflicts, she was prepared to work with the boy soldier rather than against him in order to bring her mission to a successful conclusion.

Danny moved forward, checking out the rooms to his left. Deveraux was behind him, looking right, but Danny was totally focused on what he was doing. The fire fight was just metres away on the other side of the building, but it was like something separate, another battle, or even a dream. The gunfire was strangely muffled in Danny's head, even though he could smell the cordite that was slowly creeping into every part of the building.

Danny was in automatic mode; the training was paying off. *Train hard; fight easy. Train easy, fight hard—and die.*

He was approaching the end of the corridor. One door remained, directly ahead. It was shut. Something—instinct, training, intuition, he didn't know what—was telling him that Kubara and the twins were hiding behind that closed door.

He wanted to go in first. He had to take them out. He had to see this through.

Deveraux was still a little way behind him, emerging from the last room on the right. Danny knew that once she reached him, she would insist on going in first.

Suddenly the door at the far end of the corridor burst open. Deveraux turned to see who was approaching and immediately started putting down rounds from her Sig. It was one of Kubara's men. He ducked back behind the door and Deveraux backed into the room on the right, ready to fire again if he showed his head.

Danny knew he had to make his move through the closed door. Now.

46

Danny gripped the door handle, turned it and pushed the door open with his shoulder. He saw the twins first, their petrified faces staring back at him from a few metres away.

But then he saw movement behind them and to one side. A weapon was coming up into the aim. It was all Danny needed to know. His eyes fixed on a bald head and wide eyes on top of black leather as

226

the target brought an AK up to his shoulder. Danny's brain took in the information his eyes were receiving in a split second. The twins were not a threat, he realized, but the moving head Danny was focused on could have been one of the many red balloons he'd double tapped during training.

It all happened in an instant, but for Danny it was almost like it was taking place in slow motion. He stood in the doorway, feet solid on the floor, shoulder-width apart to give the weapon a stable firing platform, left hand gripped around the right and the pistol grip. Danny's Sig was racing the AK into a firing position.

The foresight on the Sig came into focus, the bald head blurred, and Danny squeezed the trigger and double tapped the target. Both rounds entered the target's head before he had time to fire his own weapon. And this time it wasn't red chalk-dust flying through the air; it was blood.

As the target fell back, the AK clattered to the floor and skidded towards Danny.

Danny stared, knowing what he had done but not thinking about it. He was masked from the left side of the room by the open door, but the twins' horrified expressions as their eyes flicked to their right told him that someone else was there. It had to be Kubara. But why wasn't he firing?

Danny kicked the door back and turned, pistol still in the aim. Kubara was standing there, his own pistol raised.

And then Danny caught sight of Storm.

His mouth gaped open. And he hesitated.

It was enough. Kubara started to squeeze the trigger of his Makarov.

Storm screamed, '*No!*'

There was a click. A stoppage. Kubara stared at the pistol and Danny realized that he still had a chance. But before he could fire, Storm leaped in front of Kubara.

'No, Danny! No! He's my father!'

'What?!'

'It's true! I swear it! I couldn't tell you! Please! Please don't shoot him!'

Danny's mind was reeling. He heard the weapon fire from other parts of the building, but it was Storm's words that were ringing loudest in his head. It was too much to take in. Her father? It wasn't possible. It didn't make sense.

Teddy and Will were backing further into the room, away from Danny and Kubara.

'It's true!' yelled Teddy. 'Kill him!'

'Kill the bastard!' screamed Will. 'Kill him!'

Danny heard movement behind him—footsteps coming into the room—and then, before he had a chance to turn and take aim, rounds were being fired.

The twins had spoken their last words. They took rounds into the head and chest, and Deveraux kept firing until their jerking bodies hit the wall and she was almost level with Danny.

She ignored him completely; her head turned and she focused on Kubara. Danny saw that Storm was still standing in front of him, and he knew instantly that Deveraux would not ask questions; she would take them both out.

Kubara pushed his daughter away, still struggling with the mechanism of his weapon. Suddenly he gave up and lunged towards Deveraux. Instinctively, Danny flung out his right arm to slap

228

Deveraux's pistol away and put her off her aim, but as he did so, he lost his grip on his Sig and it fell to the ground.

Deveraux was momentarily off balance. Danny dived for the AK the bodyguard had carried. He focused on the forward stock and the pistol grip and rolled over on his right shoulder, gripping the weapon with both hands.

He heard the double tap as Deveraux dropped Kubara, followed by Storm's scream, and as he came up onto his knees, he saw Deveraux taking aim on her final target. Storm.

Danny fired a burst—there was no time to take aim—and Deveraux was thrown forward as the rounds entered her body.

A second later there was an explosion from the other side of the building. The door charges had been detonated: the team, or what remained of the team, was in. The automatic fire continued, but there was less of it now. It sounded as if the battle was almost won.

Danny got to his feet and dragged Storm away from the body of her father.

'You've got to go!' he yelled. 'Get out now! Back door! Quick!'

'I . . . I can't. My father . . .'

'He's dead! Go now, or they'll kill you too!'

Storm's eyes flicked back to the body of Kubara, motionless on the floor. Then she looked at Danny again for just a moment.

And then she was gone.

Danny heard her footsteps fading away along the corridor as he turned to look at Deveraux. He stood over her, sweat dripping from his face down onto hers. She had taken the rounds in her legs

229

and back. Her stomach was heaving up and down as her blood slowly oozed out, flowing onto the cold concrete floor and mingling with the dead guard's and Kubara's so that it looked as though all three were floating on a sea of red.

Deveraux remained conscious as her life slowly ebbed away, but Danny still had words he needed her to hear.

'This wasn't how I wanted it. I wanted you to suffer before I killed you. For Elena, for what you did to her, and for what you put her through, even before she died.'

Deveraux coughed, and blood appeared at one corner of her mouth. She forced herself to speak. 'Get on with it, Danny. You've won.'

Danny looked down at her and saw that her eyes were beginning to glaze over. He shook his head. 'I haven't won. Elena's still dead.'

'Just do it.'

Danny took aim at Deveraux's forehead and fired a single round.

It was over.

Somewhere in the building, a door crashed back. The automatic fire had stopped and Danny heard someone running down the corridor and a Brit shouting out orders.

He dropped the AK and stepped away from the bodies as the team entered the room. He raised both arms—he knew the drill: get his hands up so he was not deemed a threat and then identify himself.

'It's Danny! Danny! No weapon! I'm weapons free! It's Danny!'

EPILOGUE

Three months later

Fergus, Danny and Dudley walked slowly down the wide staircase; portraits of past British prime ministers stared out at them as they passed by, like a guard of honour from the pages of political history.

Marcie Deveraux had been posthumously awarded the George Cross, the highest possible honour for anyone outside the military, following her heroic actions in both Operation Meltdown and the mission to eliminate Kubara.

The citation mentioned her gallantry, her outstanding leadership and, ultimately, her death by hostile fire.

Her funeral had been a small, private affair; it had to be because of the nature of the work of the security services. The medal ceremony would, likewise, receive no press publicity, but at least it had been conducted at Number Ten, and by the Prime Minister himself.

He had presented the medal to Deveraux's grieving but dignified parents and her brother, who bore a striking resemblance to his younger sister.

Danny and Fergus had not received medals. It didn't bother them and it wasn't possible, anyway. Officially they'd played no part in Operation Meltdown. But the Prime Minister had made a point of personally thanking them, and shaking them warmly by the hand.

The even better news for Fergus was that his

days on the run as a wanted man were finally and officially over. Not that Fergus could run—he could barely walk; the walking stick he used now was going to be a permanent fixture in his life. But at least Dudley had kept his promise and the slate was wiped clean.

Fergus, Danny and Dudley had made their excuses and departed as soon as it was polite to do so. They left the Prime Minister earnestly engaged in conversation with Deveraux's brother as aides stood by, checking their watches, waiting for the moment when they could legitimately intervene and usher the PM away to his next engagement.

Danny walked ahead of his grandfather and Dudley, who were making much slower progress. He glanced at the portraits of the PMs. They all looked serious, severe, statesmanlike. And their penetrating eyes seemed to follow Danny as he passed.

He smiled. Perhaps they knew; perhaps they could penetrate his secret. But they wouldn't be telling.

The official autopsy had shown that rounds from the AK47 used by Kubara's bodyguard had killed Deveraux. No one was going to question whose finger had been on the trigger of the AK; it was obvious that they'd killed each other in the final shoot-out.

At the foot of the staircase Danny turned and glanced back at Dudley and his grandfather. Dudley looked pleased: after all, Operation Meltdown had been a total success and he had finally been allowed to take his long-deferred retirement. The knighthood would follow in the next New Year's Honours List.

The destruction of the two trucks, the Mini, the aircraft hangar, and the accompanying unfortunate deaths had been reported as a tragic accident; fires sparked by the explosion of a wartime bomb, which had lain undiscovered for more than sixty years.

Dudley had chosen the wartime bomb story. He had planned to use the 'exploding gas bottle' explanation, but the bomb seemed more fitting, almost like a tribute to the real heroes who had flown from the old airbase.

As far as the Headingham twins were concerned, they were officially listed as missing persons, last seen at a football match in Barcelona. Mummy had detectives working on the case—she wasn't going to give up the search for her beloved boys.

The Meltdown formula was gone, destroyed with its creators and their accomplices. The four trucks had been tracked across Europe by various agencies and those networks had been mopped up before the shipments were destroyed. Dudley knew that in some government laboratory, scientists would still be at work on the few remaining tablets, attempting to unravel the secrets of the manufacturing process. They would want to know, just in case some other brilliant chemist ever managed to find the answer and then pick up where the twins had left off.

But that wasn't Dudley's problem. He'd done his job. To the letter. It had all panned out perfectly.

Dudley had been obliged to remove his much-loved overcoat for the award ceremony, but as a Downing Street minion approached with the coat in his hands, Dudley smiled as if he was welcoming back a long-lost friend.

He slipped the coat on and began doing up the

233

buttons. Fergus stood at the bottom of the staircase, leaning on his walking stick, and watched.

'Four of these have seen me through my entire career,' said Dudley wistfully. 'This one has lasted thirteen—no, fourteen years.' He sighed. 'Don't think they make them any more.'

They were ushered towards the front door and Dudley led the way out into Downing Street, nodding at the uniformed police officer, who stepped aside to let them pass.

A car stood waiting by the kerb outside.

Dudley fastened the top button on his overcoat and then looked at Danny. 'A very moving and fitting ceremony, I thought.'

Danny's face gave absolutely nothing away. 'Yeah, I guess she died the way she would have wanted to.'

Dudley held his gaze briefly and then nodded. 'Yes, I'm sure you're right.' He held out his hand. 'Good luck, Danny,' he said.

'Thanks.' Danny took the outstretched hand.

Dudley turned to Fergus and they also shook hands. 'And good luck to you, Mr Watts. If you take my advice, you'll slow down a little now. We're neither of us as young as we used to be, you know.'

He glanced at the waiting car. 'Well, I'm off to the tube station. They don't stretch to cars for me now I'm officially retired.'

He nodded once more and then turned and strode purposefully away.

Danny smiled at his grandfather. 'Want a lift?'

Fergus shook his head. 'Think I'll walk for a bit. The doctor reckons I should keep this knee working as much as I can.'

They were silent for a moment, looking at each other, knowing that their long adventure was finally over and that from now on their lives would take completely different directions.

But Fergus had one final question. 'So, come on, you can tell me now—what did happen with Deveraux?'

'You know what happened,' said Danny without a flicker of emotion.

'Do I?'

'Yeah. Exactly what it says in the report.'

Fergus nodded slowly. He could have been looking at himself all those years ago. His thoughts flicked back to the many times he'd ranted and raved at his grandson about not obeying orders, not sticking to SOPs. But he knew now that he was wrong. Danny had learned well; there was nothing more he could teach him.

Fergus smiled. 'You'll keep in touch, eh?'

'When I can. You know it might be difficult sometimes.'

'Yeah, I know,' said Fergus. He reached out and wrapped his arms around his grandson and held him tightly for a few seconds. When he stepped back, Danny could see that his grandfather's eyes were moist.

'Take care, Danny,' he said quickly and then walked away.

After a few steps he called out to the figure that had almost reached the gates at the end of Downing Street. 'Dudley!'

Dudley looked back and then stopped and waited as Fergus, with the aid of his walking stick, marched towards him, like a veteran at a

Remembrance Day parade. He was showing them that, despite his injury, despite the years of conflict and action, he was still strong. He always would be.

It was all about pride—in himself, and in his grandson.

Danny watched for a few moments, then opened the passenger door of the waiting vehicle and got in.

The driver turned and looked at him. 'Go all right?'

'Yeah, it went fine.' Danny smiled. 'Prime Minister sends his regards.'

Lee laughed and started the engine, and Danny took out his mobile phone and scrolled through the saved text messages until he found the one he wanted.

Safe. Thank you. x

He knew he would never see her again; it was time to make the new start complete. He pressed the delete button.

The hydraulic steel barriers at the end of Downing Street lowered and the vehicle moved slowly out into Whitehall.

Fergus and Dudley were standing by the high black gates. They both raised a hand and waved a farewell to Danny and he nodded back at them.

And then the car turned right and pulled swiftly away, towards Thames House, the headquarters of MI5.